Sportsline
Death Vault

To Gail Penston
with thanks for her enthusiasm

Other titles by Keith Miles available in Armada

The Sportsline series

2 Fast Wheels

The Sin Bin series

Iggy
Melanie
Bev
Tariq

Sportsline
Death Vault

Keith Miles

An Armada Original

DEATH VAULT was written before the recent political upheaval in Czechoslovakia and it has been impossible to keep pace with the rapidly changing events there. We hope that our readers will make allowances for this fact and enjoy this book on its own merits as a thriller.

First published in the U.K. in 1990 in Armada

Armada is an imprint of the Children's Division, part of the Collins Publishing Group, 8 Grafton Street, London W1X 3LA.

Copyright © 1990 by Keith Miles

Phototypeset by Input Typesetting Ltd, London
Printed and bound in Great Britain by
William Collins Sons & Co. Ltd, Glasgow

Conditions of Sale
This book is sold subject to the condition that it shall not, by way of trade or otherwise, be lent, re-sold, hired out or otherwise circulated without the publisher's prior consent in any form of binding or cover other than that in which it is published and without a similar condition including this condition being imposed on the subsequent purchaser.

Chapter 1

Donna Melrose was in a state of high excitement. It was the best day of her life. She never realized what true happiness was until she woke up that morning and found the world an infinitely more beautiful place. Her dream was about to be fulfilled at last. It had been a wild hope, an impossible fantasy. Not any more. The miracle had finally happened.

As she left the house and headed for school, she was walking on air. She did not even notice the light drizzle and the gusting wind. A dull day in mid-winter was the height of summer to her. Donna's freckled face glowed. Her cheeks were flushed, her teeth bared in a broad grin and her eyes glistening with joy.

One of her friends fell in beside her.

"Hi, Donna."

"Hello, Kim."

"How can you look so cheerful?"

"What do you mean?"

"We've got Double Maths today."

"Have we?"

"Yes," moaned Kim. "And Physics. And Chem. All the crap subjects. We'll be bored rigid. So why the big smile? You look as if you've just won the pools."

"I have, Kim. In a sense."

"Eh?"

"Don't tell me you've forgotten."

"Forgotten what?"

"They're arriving this afternoon."

"Ah!" said Kim as the penny dropped. "I'm with you now. Emilie Whatsername."

"Deltchev."

"That's her. Emilie Deltchev."

Donna was exhilarated by the sheer mention of the name and she laughed involuntarily. The great passion in her life was gymnastics and her role-model was Emilie Deltchev. She could still remember the enormous thrill she got from watching the tiny Czech girl fight her way to a succession of gold medals at the recent Olympics. Emilie Deltchev was supreme.

Kim was less impressed by her achievements.

"Prefer Michael Jackson myself."

"What?"

"If I could meet anyone," said Kim airily, "I mean, anyone in the whole world, I'd choose Michael Jackson. Then Tom Cruise. Then Jason Donovan. In fact, ideally, I'd have all three together," She giggled wickedly. "They could take it in turns to ravish me."

"Trust you!"

"Well, at least we'd have fun together. That's more than Emilie Thingface can offer. Okay, she's an amazing gymnast but so what? She can't sing or dance. Can't even speak English. Why do you want to meet her?"

"Because she's wonderful."

"At what, though? The handspring vault and the asymmetric bars." Another giggle. "My three have got a talent that I could share!"

Donna pushed her playfully and they strolled on happily. She was very fond of Kim Davison even though her friend did not share her obsession with gymnastics. Kim was a tall, thin, angular girl with close-cropped fair hair and a pert face. Donna was shorter and slighter with a mop of reddish curls. Both girls were attractive enough to earn a lot of attention from the boys but Kim was the one who knew how to handle it.

"I feel so lucky!" said Donna.

"Try to keep it a secret."

"Why?"

"Because some people can get really jealous. You go bouncing into school with that stupid grin and they'll do their level best to wipe it off for you."

"Will they?"

"Think of Tania Hancox."

"Oh."

"She can be a real cow."

Donna's elation died. The advice was sound. It brought her down to earth with a bag. Friends like Kim could be relied upon to enjoy her good fortune and to wish her well. But Donna had enemies as well and they would be seething with jealousy. There was trouble ahead and it would come from one main source.

Tania Hancox.

She could wreck everything.

The Hillcrest Sports and Recreation Centre was a striking piece of architecture. It was a huge, futuristic, multi-purpose complex with an imposing frontage of mirror glass. Built in one of London's outer suburbs, it offered a wide selection of attractions. Its facilities included a swimming pool, squash courts, an indoor bowling green, a gymnasium, saunas, solaria, a lounge bar, a restaurant and a creche. The motto of Hillcrest was Sport for All.

The jewel in its crown was the main sports hall which was vast. It had a dozen courts for badminton and four for tennis. The floor was reinforced to accommodate cycling and roller-skating. Anything and everything from football to hockey was played there. Screens could be used to split the area into four quarters. When its seating was wheeled into place, the hall could be used as a venue for major sporting occasions of all kinds with a capacity audience of two thousand.

Hillcrest was a source of great pride to the local community but it was beset by many problems. Most of them were financial but some were nakedly political. This put its Director under constant pressure.

"We should have doubled the seat prices."

"People will only pay so much, Harry."

"We need to squeeze every last penny out of them."

"I prefer a full house at a lower price."

"We're underselling ourselves, Cliff."

"I don't agree."

"You have to be more realistic."

"Look," said Cliff Melrose. "Most of the spectators will be kids who got hooked on gymnastics by watching the Olympics on telly. There's a limit to how much they can afford. If we want them to come to Hillcrest, we have to keep our seat prices within their budget."

"This is a business, Cliff – not a charity."

"I know that."

"Then take a more commercial attitude."

"Let me do my job my way."

"There's public money at stake here."

"Get off my back, will you?"

"Someone has to keep on eye on you."

Cliff Melrose sighed. Ever since he took over as Director of Hillcrest, he had been having arguments with Councillor Harry Wyman. Enormous sums of public money had been invested in Hillcrest but it was not paying its way. Instead of being the instant success that everyone hoped and predicted, it was turning into a White Elephant. Many people on the Council – Harry Wyman among them – argued that they should cut their losses and sell the complex to one of the private bidders lurking in the shadows.

Hillcrest was given one last chance to prove itself. A new Director was brought in to turn the place into a going concern. Cliff Melrose had done wonders in the short time he'd been there but his progress was not fast enough for Harry Wyman. As they stood in the middle of the sports hall, the Councillor issued another warning.

"Time is running out, Cliff."

"You gave me a full year."

"Make more use of it."

"I'm doing my best."

"That's a matter of opinion."

"We'll just have to agree to differ, Harry."

"What do you mean?"

"I actually want Hillcrest to survive."

"So do I."

"Pull the other one."

"I was behind this project from the start," said the Councillor with easy pomposity. "Ask anyone. I helped to create this building."

"Then why are you trying to sell it off?"

"It's an option we have to consider."

"Only if we fail."

"Which is what you are doing."

Cliff Melrose looked him accusingly in the eye.

"Isn't that what you want?"

Harry Wyman spluttered helplessly for a few seconds then turned on his heel and stalked off. Cliff watched him go. Wyman was a fat, sleek, grey-haired man in a smart suit. He had a powerful voice in Council affairs and had to be humoured but Cliff Melrose could only take so much of him. His job was difficult enough as it was without having people like Harry Wyman baying at his heels.

Cliff looked around the hall. It had already been set up for the big event. England versus Czechoslovakia. Hillcrest was to play host to some of the finest women gymnasts in the world. It had been a real coup to get the international match staged at the complex and Cliff took great satisfaction from it. He was very conscious of just how much was hanging on the success of the occasion. It had to be a financial as well as a sporting triumph and it was vital to generate good publicity for Hillcrest.

To make sure that it all went smoothly, Cliff Melrose was supervising everything personally. He was a stocky, muscular man of middle height with a shock of red hair which both his children had inherited and which acted as a kind of early warning system for the explosive temper that he could sometimes unleash. A former professional soccer player, Cliff kept himself exceptionally fit and more or less lived in a track suit.

His new job was a real challenge but he accepted it with characteristic zeal.

There was one consolation. He was able to answer his daughter's most fervent prayer and he was delighted about that. Donna worshipped Emilie Deltchev. Thanks to her father, she would now have the chance to meet her face to face. Cliff chuckled to himself. Hillcrest gave him endless headaches but it did come up with the odd bonus.

That made it all worthwhile.

They landed at Heathrow and cleared Customs without any undue problems. As they pushed their luggage trolleys into the Arrivals Lounge, the visitors got their first taste of the British press. A dozen or more reporters and photographers were waiting to pounce. Czechoslovakia had sent a team of eight girls under the care of a manager, a coach and a fearsome-looking woman who acted as surrogate mother and official minder but the newshounds were only interested in one person. They closed in.

"Hello, Emilie!"
"Welcome to England!"
"What have you got lined up for us?"
"Anything new?"
"Glad to be here?"
"Smile, Emilie."
"Flash those teeth."
"Come on, Em."
"Big, big smile."
"Hold it there!"

All of the gymnasts were relatively short but Emilie Deltchev was by far the smallest. She had a gamine charm that the cameras loved and she turned it on obligingly. Emilie beamed happily in the way that won her millions of fans around the world during the Olympics. There was an elfin radiance about her that was quite irresistible. Some of the other girls were clearly peeved and resentful at the attention she was getting but there was nothing that they could do about it. Emilie Deltchev was a star. Her famous smile would be plastered all over the morning papers on the following day.

"Just one more, Emilie!"
"Turn your head to the right."
"Lift your chin a bit."
"Brush your hair back."
"Don't move."
"That's terrific!"
"Thanks, Emilie."

Understanding only part of what was said to her, she reacted instinctively and gave them what they wanted. But her mind was not on the photo session. As the commands came thick and fast and the cameras flashed away, Emilie moved her head so that she could gaze around the lounge with quickening interest. There was a glorious sparkle in her large, brown eyes.

She was looking for someone.

Tania Hancox stayed her hand until mid-afternoon. She had several opportunities to bait Donna Melrose but she let them pass, preferring to wait until they all went down to the school gymnasium. That was the best place to attack. It was also the most appropriate.

"Gymnastics is rubbish!" she began.
"No, it isn't," said Donna.

"It's for wimps who're no good at hockey."
"You're useless at both, Tania Hancox!"
"Almost as bad as you."
"I've passed all my grades in gymnastics."
"Only 'cos you're the Teacher's Pet!"

Donna reddened and took no heed of the warning elbow that Kim jabbed in her ribs. Tania Hancox was an expert. She knew exactly how to goad Donna and subjected her to a mocking smirk. What was even more annoying was that it was almost impossible to rattle Tania herself. She won arguments for the simple reason that she could remain calm and collected. Insults seemed to wash off her. It was if she had no feelings to hurt.

"You'll grow out of it," said Tania.
"Out of what?"
"That kids' stuff in the gym."
"It's not kids' stuff!"
"Wait till you're a real woman."
"Like you, I suppose!" sneered Donna.

"At least I know what life is all about," boasted the other, striking a pose in her leotard to show off her shapely figure. "I get my exercise with my boyfriends. And I'll tell you this for nothing – it's a lot more fun than gymnastics!"

There was a flurry of giggles from the knot of girls who had gathered around to watch the row. Donna Melrose was easily the most talented gymnast in the group and this made her a regular target for Tania's sniping. The latter had all the advantages in any quarrel. She was older, taller, more mature and much more self-confident. Also – and this was the unkindest cut – Tania Hancox was genuinely beautiful. Her stunning features were set off by long black hair and long, lustrous eyelashes that she could flutter with consummate skill. It enabled her to attract almost any boy she chose and it gave Donna yet another reason to hate her classmate.

One of those smitten was her own brother.

Stuart Melrose.

Tania stepped in to resume the attack.

"When's that little twerp coming?"

"What twerp?"

"Emilie Deathface."

"Deltchev!" corrected Donna. "And she's not a twerp. She happens to be a world champion."

"So am I – at some things!"

"Why don't you shut your mouth?" said Kim bravely.

"Keep out of this," ordered Tania.

"Then leave Donna alone."

"Why? Can't she fight her own battles?"

"You're only jealous of her."

"You've got to be joking!"

Tania looked at Donna with such withering scorn that the latter almost blushed. Petite and defenceless in her leotard, she was only too aware of how much younger and inexperienced she was than her enemy. Donna had a lithe body that could move with balletic grace but she did sometimes yearn for a fuller figure. Standing next to the voluptuous Tania, she felt like a child.

Kim forgot her own earlier advice. Seeing that her friend was in trouble, she stepped in loyally to support her once again.

"Donna's going to meet Emilie."

"Big deal!" said Tania with a curl of the lip.

"Her father's arranged it for her."

"Thank you, Daddy!"

"It's more than anyone'd do for you."

"That's where you're wrong, Kim Davison," said Tania, inspecting her painted fingernails before shining them on her sleeve. "As a matter of fact, I'm going to have a chat with the little twerp myself. Woman to woman."

"No, you're not!" yelled Donna.

"I've got a boyfriend who'll fix it up."

"Who?"

"Your brother – Stuart."

"Don't you dare!"

Donna lost control and flung herself at Tania but the tussle was over before it began. Jane Ryder, the tall, young PE mistress, came bursting into the changing room and clapped her hands for attention. The two combatants parted guiltily as the teacher came over to them.

"What's going on here?"

"Nothing, Miss Ryder," said Tania.

"Nothing, Miss Ryder," echoed Donna.

The teacher could guess what had happened. If there was any trouble with the group, it usually centred around Tania Hancox. She gave the girl a reproving stare but she got only a defiant grin in return. Donna, by contrast, stood there in a welter of embarrassment. The last thing she wanted was to upset her favourite teacher.

"Right," said Jane Ryder briskly. "Let's forget it. Into the gym, everyone. We've got work to do."

The girls ran quickly out into the corridor.

The PE mistress did not spare them. Knowing the importance of a proper warm-up period, she devoted half the lesson to a series of running, skipping, bending and stretching exercises. Only when her group was thoroughly loosened up did she allow them near the apparatus. They began with vaults. Jane Ryder positioned herself so that she could help any of the girls who lost their balance as they came over the horse. Each vault in the sequence was slightly more difficult than the last.

Donna acquitted herself well but she was only going through the motions. Her mind was in a turmoil. She was desperate to keep Emilie Deltchev to herself. The thought that Tania Hancox might worm her way into Hillcrest was agonizing, all the more so as she would use Stuart to get there. Donna and her brother had their differences but she could not believe he would do anything this cruel to her. Or would he?

"Right, girls, let's move over here."

Jane Ryder took them across to the beam and motioned for them to sit down on the floor. Tania was panting. She had not enjoyed the vaulting and was glad of the rest. Donna took care to sink down well away from her but she was not allowed to stay there for long.

The teacher went through her weekly catechism.

"To be a good gymnast, you need four main things," she said. "What are they?"

"Two arms and two legs," said Tania.

"No," replied Jane over the giggles. "Strength. Stamina. Suppleness. Skill. And I'm bound to observe, that you didn't show much of any of them,

Tania. You went over that vaulting horse like a sack of potatoes."

The giggles were turned against the pupil this time. Donna and Kim joined in with glee. Tania shrugged it off.

"Those four things are not enough," continued the teacher. "You can have strength, stamina, suppleness, skill and yet you still won't be a champion. You need something else. Something special to set you apart from the others. In a word – Style." She turned to Donna. "Show them."

"Me, Miss Ryder?"

"Who else? You're the only girl with real style."

"Yes, Miss."

"Off you go, then. A demonstration."

Under any other circumstances, Donna would have leapt at the chance to display her skills but she was simply not in the mood. Her head was still buzzing with what Tania had said to her and she was unable to concentrate.

"Don't keep us waiting," said Jane Ryder pleasantly.

"Go on, Donna!" urged Kim enthusiastically.

"Yes!" said another girl.

And there was general encouragement from the others.

Donna approached the beam and took a deep breath. It was a difficult piece of apparatus and she would have to proceed with the utmost care. Balance and precision were absolutely crucial. She tried hard to focus her mind on the routine she had practised with such dedication.

She stood on the springboard in front of the beam

and jumped to front support, swinging her right leg over the timber so that she finished in a saddle sit position with both legs stretched behind. A swift movement brought her knee up on to the beam, then she was tripping along it on her toes, pivoting, jumping, then winning applause with a forward somersault that was perfectly timed. Then she went down into V-sit, swinging her legs back until she was lying on her front, bending her left leg so that her toe pointed towards her head.

Jane Ryder looked on with approval. Donna was now starting to show the individual style which marked her out as a true gymnast. The longer the routine went on, the more assured and daring she became. Her movement had a graceful fluidity that was mesmerizing. As she came to the climax of her routine, she summoned up all her nerve and commitment to execute a backward somersault but her concentration faltered at the last moment. She spun through the air but missed the beam with her feet and came down hard on her bottom before falling heavily to the rubber mat below.

There was a stunned silence.

Then Tania Hancox led the derisive laughter.

Donna was mortified.

The hotel window commanded an excellent view of the surroundings. From his vantage point on the fourth floor, the man with the hornrimmed spectacles could look right down the main street to Hillcrest itself. He paused to note what a hideous building it really was then congratulated himself on choosing the perfect room.

So far, everything had gone to plan.

The arrival of the minibus took his eyes downwards again. As the vehicle pulled up on the forecourt of the hotel, the commissionaire scurried out to open its door. The manager was the first person out of the minibus. Then came the girls, staring up at the hotel with candid awe, gasping, pointing, trying to take in its full wonder in one almighty gulp. Their accommodation in Prague was nowhere near as luxurious as this.

Emilie Deltchev was as impressed as the others. Her face lit up for an instant then she was hurried inside the building with the others.

The man on the fourth floor had seen enough. He reached inside his coat and took out his gun. After checking that it was loaded, he slipped it back into its holster then sat down in a chair.

They had finally arrived.

He was ready.

Chapter 2

Maggie Melrose spotted the signs at once. When her son came home from school and went straight upstairs to take a bath, she knew that something was up. Stuart Melrose was a tall, thin, lackadaisical youth with the family freckles. Now in the first-year sixth at Kingsmead Comprehensive, he was an amiable, easy-going, hopelessly untidy character who liked to saunter through life. A new urgency had now been injected into him. When he finally emerged from the bathroom, he looked so clean and smart that Maggie was taken aback. Quite unnecessarily, he had given himself a shave with his father's razor and incurred two small cuts on his chin. As he popped into the kitchen to tell his mother that he would not be staying for tea, there was a glazed look in his eye.

The evidence was overwhelming. Maggie Melrose was a kind and understanding mother who liked to be involved in her children's lives. She gave him a warm smile and offered him the chance to confide in her.

"What's her name?"
"Eh?"
"I'm not blind, Stuart."
"Dunno what you're on about."
"The bath. The shave. The transformation."
"I wanted to smarten up, that's all."
"For whose benefit, though?"

"My own," he said with a dismissive shrug.

"You can't fool me."

"Not trying to, Mum."

"See it from my point of view," she said reasonably. "One son goes into the bathroom and a totally different one comes out. There has to be a reason."

"Yeah. I'm going out with the lads."

"Pull the other one!"

"You'll have to excuse me."

And before she could press him any further, Stuart trotted off up to his bedroom to put the final touches to his appearance. Maggie grinned and carried on getting the tea. She was a slim, attractive woman with fair hair. Like her husband, she worked at Hillcrest where she was the resident physiotherapist. While Cliff Melrose was blunt and outspoken, however, his wife was quiet and patient. At work and at home, they made a very effective team.

Maggie pottered about the kitchen, wondering who could have wrought such a change in her son. She did not have to wait long for an answer. The front door opened then slammed and Donna came racing into the kitchen. Her face was purple with rage.

"Where is he?" she demanded.

"Who?"

"That traitor!"

"Calm down, Donna."

"I'll kill him when I get my hands on him."

"Stuart?"

"Dirty, rotten, stinking – "

"What on earth is he supposed to've done?"

"Betrayed me. With that cow."

"Who are you talking about?"

"Tania Hancox."

"Ah!" said Maggie as light dawned. "So it's her."

"She waited for him after school then jumped on him. Stuart thinks she actually likes him but she's only using him to get back at me."

"Slow down a minute, Donna."

"It's true, Mum. She wants him to get her in to meet Emilie Deltchev and it's not fair! Emilie is mine. I've been waiting for this for months. I don't want Tania Hancox to horn in on it. She doesn't even like gymnastics."

Donna's rage changed to sadness and Maggie saw that she was on the verge of tears. Taking her daughter in her arms, she patted her on the back and made soothing noises. Just as Donna was allowing herself to be comforted, feet were heard descending the staircase. The girl erupted again. Darting into the hall, she confronted her brother.

"You pig, Stuart Melrose!"

"What have I done now?" he said innocently.

"As if you didn't know."

"I don't, honestly."

"Taking sides against your own sister!"

"Why don't we discuss this sensibly?" said Maggie, who had come into the hall. "Let's all go into the living room and sit down."

"No time, Mum," said Stuart.

"He has to get over to Tania's house!" said Donna.

"Shut up, will you?"

"When she calls, he goes running."

"Bickering will get us nowhere," said Maggie.

"Who's bickering?" said Stuart, opening the door.

"I don't want an argument. I've got somewhere to go."

"Don't bring her to Hillcrest!" howled Donna.

"I'll do what I like," he replied.

"You dare!" she warned. "If Tania Hancox spoils my big moment, I'll never speak to you as long as I live."

Stuart waved a goodbye to his mother then ducked out quickly to avoid any further embarrassment. Donna slammed the door vengefully after him.

She had got her message across.

The Czechoslovakian team were staying on the tenth floor of the hotel. Since they were on the north side of the building, they faced central London and could pick out some of the taller landmarks in the distance. It was the first time most of them had been to Britain and they were very excited. Everything seemed to be bigger, better and more modern than in their own country.

Emilie Deltchev was more pleased than any of them to be there. All the team were still in their teens but she was at once the youngest and the tiniest. She had been assigned to a room with Zuzana Sotornik, her one real friend among the girls, but there were some things that she could not even share with her. When Zuzana slipped out of the room, therefore, Emilie immediately reached into her suitcase and took out the book that was hidden under some clothing. Published in her native city of Prague, it held her spellbound for half an hour.

Then there was a tap on the door and she hastily put the book under the pillow. The door opened to admit the ample figure of Terezie Klimenko, the heavily-built woman who acted as the team's bodyguard and unofficial mascot. Terezie could be tough and uncompromising when any of her charges were under threat but she could also be soft and maternal. Emilie liked her. The older woman was amusing company when you got to know her properly.

They spoke in Czech.

"Ready?" asked Terezie.

"Where are we going?"

"To look at the Hillcrest Centre."

"Is that where we'll be competing?"

"Yes, Emilie. In front of a large crowd. There will be a lot of journalists there. We must do well so that they write good reports about us. That will be a great help to our country."

"I know," said Emilie wistfully.

"We must always put Czechoslavakia first."

The girl nodded and reached into the wardrobe for her coat. Terezie took her out into the corridor to join the others. They were soon packing themselves into the lift in a solid wedge. When they reached the ground floor, they walked across the hotel foyer and went out through the main doors. None of them saw the man who was sitting in a corner and pretending to read a newspaper through his hornrimmed glasses.

He got up casually and followed them out.

The Melrose family were certainly committed to Hillcrest. Not only did Cliff and Maggie work there but their children used the facilities on a regular basis. The fifth member of the household treated the place like a home from home. Wilf Melrose, a retired railwayman, was a former county bowls champion and he loved to practice on the indoor green during the autumn and winter months. Now in his seventies, Wilf was starting to show his age and, since the death of his wife, he had become much more irascible. His red hair had retreated to a pale fringe around his bald head but there was no mistaking the facial likeness between him and his son.

"Not now, Dad," said Cliff.

"But I want to make a formal complaint."

"Save it till we get home."

"This concerns Hillcrest."

"Sorry. It'll have to wait."

"Oh," said Wilf huffily. "Too busy to listen to your own father, are you?"

"Of course not. But I've got a lot on my plate right now. The Czech team is about to arrive any moment and I have to show them around."

"So I take second place to a bunch of Commies!"

"They're world-famous gymnasts, Dad."

"I don't care who they are. I want my say."

And Wilf chuntered on about some incident that had happened earlier on the indoor bowling green. Cliff was relieved when Donna came running in through the door.

"They're here, Dad!"

"Great!"

"Emilie Deltchev is with them. I saw her."

"What about my bowls?" complained Wilf.

"Forget 'em for the time being," said Cliff firmly. "This takes precedence over everything."

Wilf cursed mutinously but he went unheard.

Donna glanced quickly around the sports hall then grabbed her father by the elbow.

"Stuart's not here, is he?"

"No."

"Has he been in touch?"

"Yes. Rang me up. Wanted to bring some girl here."

"Tania Hancox."

"I told him it's not on. The Czech team is coming to size the place up. They don't want to be bothered with strangers. Family is different. But I'm not letting just anyone get in on the act."

"You're marvellous, Dad!" said Donna, planting a big kiss on his cheek. "I should have known you'd help me."

Before Cliff could reply, the door opened and the visitors were ushered in. He swept across to greet them. The party was led by Viktor Zaremba, the team manager, and his wife, Ludmila, who was the coach. Both in their late thirties, they were an arresting pair, lean, bronzed and exuding fitness. Cliff could remember the time when both of them had been Olympic stars themselves.

Viktor introduced him to each member of the team and to the watchful Terezie Klimenko. When Cliff indicated his daughter and father, the visitors waved cheerily to them. Donna was thrilled when Emilie flashed her a smile.

"Isn't she wonderful!" said Donna.

"Reds!" muttered Wilf.

"She's brilliant, Grandad!"

"Bet I could beat her on the bowling green."

Cliff now conducted the team around the sports hall

to show them the apparatus. As he talked away, Terezie took on the role of translator and made sure that the girls did not miss anything of what he said. Donna drifted across to join the group and worked her way close to Emilie. Simply being in the same building as her idol gave her an electric charge. She was overtaken by a sense of euphoria.

Viktor stressed that the training sessions were strictly private. He did not want his gymnasts bothered by the press or by any unwanted spectators. Cliff assured him that all his wishes would be met. During the two days before the competition, they could have unlimited use of the sports hall and keys to lock the doors against any intrusion. The visitors seemed pleased with what they found and started to relax.

Donna chose the moment to prompt her father.

"The interview," she whispered.

"Oh, yes." He turned to Viktor. "Mr Zaremba, I know that you don't want to be badgered by journalists but I wonder if I could ask you a favour?"

"Please do."

"My daughter writes for the school newspaper. On the sports pages. We wondered if it would be at all possible for her to have a short interview with Emilie?"

"Ten minutes is all I'd need," said Donna, seeing the doubts on the manager's face. "I promise not to be a nuisance. And I'd show you my story before it was printed so you could make any changes. It won't interrupt your training schedule. I could interview her at the hotel."

Before Viktor could answer with a polite refusal, another voice piped up. It was Emilie Deltchev. She caught the gist of what Donna was saying and was only too happy to cooperate.

"Yes," she said, beaming away. "I like."

Viktor and Ludmila lapsed back into Czech to discuss the matter and they still had reservations but Emilie was not to be deflected. She argued with them in her native tongue and they eventually bowed to her wishes.

"Okay," agreed Viktor. "Tomorrow. Ten minutes."
"Thank you!" gushed Donna.
She was ecstatic.

Watching it all from the rear of the balcony, the two of them lurked in the shadows. Tania Hancox was fractious.

"This is no blooming good!"
"I got you in, didn't I?" said Stuart.
"Only by smuggling me up the fire exit. I wanted to do what your sister's doing. Meet them properly."
"Dad wouldn't allow it."
"But you promised, Stuart."
"I tried."
"You should have insisted."
"No point. He put his foot down."
"Stand up to him."
"You don't know Dad."
"I thought you could get me down there with Donna," she said irritably. "Hiding away up here is no fun."
"Shhh!"
"What's up now?"
"They'll hear us."

Stuart was in a quandary. Anxious to please Tania,

he was just as keen to avoid being seen by his father. If Cliff knew that the girl had been sneaked in against his express wishes, he would be furious and Stuart did not want to risk that. Crouching down in the half-dark, Tania nudged one of the chairs and made it squeak. Everyone down below looked up into the balcony. Stuart lost his nerve. Keeping low all the time, he grabbed Tania by the elbow and hustled her out through the door.

In the passageway outside, they got a shock. They barged straight into a tall, well-dressed man who was wearing hornrimmed spectacles. He gave an apologetic smile and spoke in cultured tones.

"I do beg your pardon. Is the bar this way?"

A light meal back at the hotel helped the gymnasts to feel more at home, and they were laughing and joking as they went upstairs. Viktor warned them to let nobody but Terezie to their rooms and she herself made a final tour of inspection before turning in for an early night. Emilie chatted with her room mate for an hour or so then Zuzana drifted off to sleep. After making sure that her companion would not wake up again, Emilie reached under the pillow for the book which she had been reading in secret. By the light of the bedside lamp, she dipped into it again and soon became quite immersed. Every so often she would mouth a phrase or sentence in English.

When she at last put the book aside and switched off the light, one line in particular stayed in her mind. She stared up into the darkness and whispered softly.

"I love your country . . . "

Tania Hancox mellowed. When Stuart took her to a nearby coffee bar and treated her to a snack, she began to accept that the date was not a complete failure. She liked him. It was obvious that he liked her far more but she was accustomed to that with boys. They drooled over her. It gave her a feeling of power and she enjoyed taking full advantage of it.

She sipped her coffee and fluttered her eyelashes.

"What would you do for me, Stuart?"

"Anything!"

"Do you mean that?"

"Just put me to the test."

"I did. You blew it."

"Forget what happened at Hillcrest," he said. "Give me the chance to make it up to you."

"Okay. Tell me about Donna."

"Who?"

"Donna, you idiot. Your sister."

"We don't want to talk about her."

"I do."

"Why?"

"Because I'm interested. In her. In you. In the whole Melrose family."

"Is that true, Tania?"

"Of course." She ran a hand gently down his arm to coax him. "Come on, Stuart. I want to know. Tell me all."

"Well . . . all right."

They stayed for well over an hour while she pumped him about his sister then they walked back to her house. She was so pleased with the ammunition he had unwittingly given her that she let him kiss her a few times at the doorstep. Then she eased him away.

"Can I see you again, Tania?"

"Probably."

"When?"

"Who knows?"

"It was a fantastic evening."

"Thanks, Stuart."

She gave him a last peck on the cheek and sent him off in a state of sublime happiness. Boys were such ridiculous creatures. It took so little to ensnare them. She sniggered to herself then let herself into the house.

Her father was in the living room with her uncle. Both gave her a welcome then her father went off to pour another couple of drinks. When her uncle asked her about her evening, Tania started to talk about Hillcrest. His ears pricked up at once and he questioned her closely about Cliff Melrose. She was able to feed him all sorts of gossip that Stuart had let fall and her uncle was plainly fascinated by it.

"Are you seeing him again?" he asked.

"Dunno. He's a bit dull."

"I'll make it worth your while, Tania."

"To go out with Stuart Melrose?"

"Yes," he said. "Find out more about his father. Get me anything you can about the way Hillcrest is run. Think you could do that for me?"

"I suppose so."

"Then have this on account."

He took out his wallet and gave her five pounds.

"Thanks, Uncle Harry!" she said.

"I can't pay enough for good information."

"You'll get it, don't worry."

Councillor Harry Wyman smirked.

He now had a spy in the enemy camp.

Chapter 3

The magic had not worn off by morning. Donna Melrose was up at the crack of dawn to go through her notes and to prepare herself for the interview. She was actually going to have a private conversation with Emilie Deltchev, albeit through an interpreter. It was more than she had dared to hope. Her school newspaper would print her exclusive on the front page of their next issue. Everyone would see it. The article would gain her prestige and give a nasty jolt to the egregious Tania Hancox. It would serve her right for trying to steal Donna's thunder.

When Maggie Melrose came down in a housecoat to make the breakfast, she found her daughter hunched over the table with the kitchen scissors in her hand.

"Donna, what are you doing?"

"Cutting out this photo of Emilie."

"But that's today's paper. Nobody's read it yet."

"I need the picture, Mum."

Donna held up the large photograph of Emilie. It had been taken at Heathrow the previous day and showed her beaming happily at the camera. The caption fell back on a now familiar pun – THE BOUNCING CZECH. Donna put the photo carefully into her file. Later on, she would paste it into her scrapbook along with everything else she had collected about her little heroine.

Maggie held up the newspaper and peered through the window that had been cut out by the scissors. She heaved a mock sigh.

"Your grandad won't like this one bit."

"He grumbles about everything."

"You know what he'll say, don't you?"

"Oh, yes!" Donna deepened her voice to give a passable imitation of Wilf. "Vandalism, that's what it is!"

They shared a laugh then Maggie turned to the stove.

"What would you like for breakfast?"

"Had it an hour ago, Mum."

"I see."

"Wanted to get off early this morning," said Donna. "Did I tell you that she's only half-Czech?"

"Emilie Deltchev?"

"Yes. Her mother was French. In fact, her parents split up not long after she was born and her mother's brought her up on her own. So Emilie is probably more French than Czech."

"Try telling that to the Czech government," said Maggie wryly. "They've turned the poor girl into a national symbol. Must put enormous pressure on her."

"That's one of the questions I want to ask."

"She's been doing gymnastics since she was six."

"Five, actually," said Donna who knew every detail of Emilie's career. "You can't start too young if you want to get right to the top."

"Think of all the sacrifices she had to make."

"It was worth it, Mum. She's number one."

"Emilie's missed out on so much in life."

"I don't think so."

"How can she have had a normal childhood if she's been doing gymnastics all day and every day? I mean, there's just no time left for anything else." She glanced across at her daughter. "Put it this way. Would you like to be on the kind of treadmill that she is?"

Donna did not have to weigh up her reply.

"Of course. I'd love it."

The autograph hunters who waited outside Hillcrest were disappointed. They were not even allowed to thrust their books and pens at the visiting celebrities. Using her bulk and showing great purpose, Terezie Klimenko more or less bulldozed a way through the small crowd and led the gymnasts into the building. A security man then conducted them to the sports hall. Once they were inside, all doors were promptly locked. The Czechoslovakians liked to train in secret. They would not reveal their mysteries until Saturday when the paying public came to see them take on the English team.

Discipline was the watchword. Viktor Zaremba was a martinet who kept an iron control over the team. His wife, Ludmila, could be equally firm and she pushed the girls hard during every session. Gymnastics was not something which they did for enjoyment. It was a serious business and winning was paramount.

Viktor gave them his standard pep talk. His approach was totally professional. Ludmila backed him up.

"And remember," she said. "You are representing your country. If you fail on Saturday, you will not only be letting yourselves down. You will be doing a disservice to Czechoslovakia."

The girls nodded soulfully then went to work.

They spent almost three-quarters of an hour warming up with a whole variety of exercises then they divided up into four couples. One pair moved to the beam, another to the vaulting horse and another to the asymmetric bars. Emilie Deltchev and Zuzana Sotornik practiced with floor exercises. To the sound of Russian classical music, they went through their elaborate routines, polishing and refining them until they were near-perfect. Zuzana's piece was from Tchaikovsky's Nutcracker Suite but Emilie was performing to some Prokofiev.

Reputation was no source of protection. Emilie might be the Olympic champion but she still came in for severe criticism from Ludmila.

"Higher, Emilie. And point those toes more."

"I'm sorry."

"Your timing is right out this morning."

To any other observer, the Czech girl had just given a dazzling display but Ludmila saw faults in it. She made Emilie strive hard until she had rectified them. After a while, the couples rotated so that they could work on a different piece of apparatus. They began afresh.

When the morning session was finally over, the girls ran off to take a restorative shower. Zuzana let the hot water cascade down over her body.

"It doesn't get any easier, does it?"

"Mm?" Emilie was not listening.

"Ludmila knows how to crack the whip."

"Ah, yes."

"Just like a ringmaster in a circus."

"It's the only way."

"I know," agreed Zuzana. "But I do wish that we could take it easy sometimes. Have some fun. Do you know what I mean?"

Emilie nodded and gave an enigmatic smile.

She knew only too well.

The Czechoslovakian team had had a productive morning at Hillcrest and they were delighted with the facilities. Cliff Melrose was having a less happy time at his place of work. Seated behind the desk in his office, he had yet another heated exchange with his chief critic.

"It was the least I could do, Harry."

"Why didn't you clear it with us first?"

"Because I'm the Director here. I can't come running to the Council every time I have a problem. As long as I'm in charge, I'll make my own decisions."

"This was an exceptional case."

"They needed extra security."

"Why?" protested Harry Wyman. "They're only a bunch of girls. Anybody'd think they were royalty."

"In gymnastic terms, they are."

"Don't quibble."

"I had to guarantee them full security in order to get them here. It's always the same with these Communist countries. Their teams don't feel safe unless you surround them with an armed guard."

"Look how much it's costing us, though!"

"We have to spend money to make it, Harry."

"All you've done so far is to throw it away," said the Councillor, getting into his stride. "You close the sports hall for three days so that the Czechs can have unrestricted use of it and what happens? We lose all the revenue we'd get from the badminton and tennis courts. And we upset regular customers into the bargain."

"It was unavoidable."

"Not in my view."

"Maybe," said Cliff vehemently, "but you don't run Hillcrest. I know what I'm doing so why the hell don't you just let me get on with it?"

Cliff paused to take a sip of tea from the cup in front of him. He was never pleased to hear from Harry Wyman but this morning's row was particularly unpleasant. Four additional security men had been drafted in during the VIPs' stay. Knowing that the Councillor would object to the expense, Cliff had taken care not to mention his action. Harry Wyman had somehow found out.

"And another thing," droned the voice in his ear.

"What now?"

"A little bird tells me your daughter was part of the welcoming committee last night. If security is supposed to be that tight, how come she and your father managed to breach it? You were supposed to impress the Czechs with the way you'd organised things – not play Happy Families!"

"Is that all you have to say, Harry?"

"No, there's plenty more."

"Save it for another time."

"I haven't finished yet."

"Goodbye."

"Don't you dare hang up on me!"

"I've got a job to do."

Cliff Melrose slammed down the receiver and sat back in his chair. It had been a gruelling ten minutes and he felt quite frazzled. What hurt him most was the fact that Harry Wyman had got hold of so much inside information.

Cliff ran a hand through his hair.

"Who was that little bird?"

Tania Hancox bided her time until she could cause maximum humiliation. She waited until the lunch break when most of the pupils filed into the school canteen at Kingsmead. It was a large, low, echoing room with Formica tables and plastic chairs. Donna Melrose was sitting as usual with Kim Davison. Both were munching happily away when Tania Hancox rolled up with a few of her cronies. She plonked herself down in a seat opposite Donna and put her plate on the table. Her friends sat beside her. Donna could tell that they had come to poke fun at her and she vowed that she would remain cool and unflustered this time.

Tania swept aside that vow with ease.

"How's the Tooth Fairy?"

Donna's face went crimson instantly.

"Buzz off, Tania," said Kim.

"I want to speak to Tooth Fairy."

"I haven't a clue what you're on about," said Donna weakly. "So shove off and bother someone else."

"But nobody else still believes in Tooth Fairies," continued Tania, rubbing salt in the wound. "But you do. Only last week, you had a tooth taken out and left it under your pillow. Didn't you?"

Donna was mortified. It had been no more than a

family joke. She knew quite well that there were no fairies but she went through the old ritual out of fun. Her mother had left a pound under her pillow. In the Melrose household, it had given them all a laugh. In the hands of Tania Hancox, it became a weapon that could be used against her. The other girl raised her voice so that everyone on the neighbouring tables could hear.

"Donna Melrose believes in Tooth Fairies!"

There was a sudden burst of derisive laughter.

Tania Hancox set up the chant.

"Tooth Fairy! Tooth Fairy! Tooth Fairy!"

Others took it up and it spread like wildfire.

"Tooth Fairy! Tooth Fairy! Tooth Fairy!"

The whole canteen seemed to be ridiculing Donna. She bit her lip and tried to block the sound out of her ears but it built to a crescendo. Everyone was mocking her and beating the tables in time to the chant.

"Tooth Fairy! Tooth Fairy! Tooth Fairy!"

Unable to stand it any longer, she got to her feet and ran out of the canteen. A raucous cheer went up.

Tania Hancox was well-pleased with her work.

"Now I can enjoy my lunch."

The man in the hornrimmed spectacles sat at the desk in his hotel room and pored over the sheet of paper. During his brief stay, he had not wasted any time. His research had been thorough and he was convinced that his plan was foolproof. There was a tap on the door. He checked his watch and saw that his visitor was punctual. That was good. From this point on, everything had to be done strictly to time. There could be no margin for error.

He opened the door to admit a younger man. Both of them wore expensive suits and looked like businessmen of some sort. The newcomer had a moustache. It lifted as he gave a dutiful smile.

"Is everything in order?" he asked.

"More or less."

"Any problems?"

"Nothing insurmountable."

"Escape route?"

"All set up."

"Transport?"

"Standing by."

"The rest is up to us, then."

"Yes," said the man in the glasses.

"Should be a doddle."

"If we stick to plan."

"It's always gone like clockwork before."

"Only because I've set it up properly."

"When do we move in?"

"This evening."

"Right," said the newcomer. He patted the gun that was in a holster under his coat. "I've come armed."

"As ordered."

"Are we likely to use our guns?"

The other man removed his glasses to clean them. "Probably."

Stuart Melrose was so shattered that he had to sit down on a wall. He felt as if he had just stepped on a land-mine and been blown to smithereens. As he came out of school with his Adidas bag over his shoulder, Donna had ambushed him and flung a whole series of accusations at him. When he tried to defend himself, she had grabbed his bag and started to hit him with it. Stuart's pride was severely wounded. Since he had joined the sixth form, he had tried to be more cool and sophisticated and laid back. Being attacked in public by a hysterical younger sister did no good at all to his image. Donna had done wilful damage to what he called his street cred.

At the same time, she obviously had cause for her frenzy. He had given Tania Hancox the stick with which to beat Donna and that made him feel guilty. It also made him see his night out with Tania in a new light.

"Hello, Stuart."

"Ah."

"You okay?"

"No."

"What's up?"

"As if you didn't know!"

It was Tania Hancox herself, pouting sweetly at him and looking as if butter would not melt in her mouth. He hauled himself up from the wall.

"Why did you have a go at Donna?" he asked.

"It was only for a giggle."

"Some giggle! She almost murdered me."

"Donna's too sensitive, that's her trouble."

"What I told you was strictly between us, Tania."

"I know."

"Then why did you tease my sister about it?"

"The other girls egged me on."

"That's not the way she tells it?"

"Who're you going to believe – her or me?"

Stuart was thrown back on the defensive. He was being presented with a choice that he did not wish to make. His first loyalty was to his sister and he was very annoyed that something he had divulged had been used against Donna. At the same time, he was still strongly attracted to Tania and did not want to alienate her completely. Taking her out the previous evening had done wonders for his ego and for his prestige. He had been the envy of the Lower Sixth. As she stood there, hands on her hips and body arched provocatively, he could not find the words to condemn her.

Tania changed her tack and put a consolatory arm around his shoulder. Her voice became a soothing purr.

"I'm sorry, Stuart."

"Donna really goes mad when she's roused."

"Was it that bad?"

"Like being trampled by a herd of buffalo."

"I didn't mean to land you in it."

"Well, you did. Splat! Right in the middle."

"Does that mean you've gone off me?"

"Uh, no . . . well . . . "

"I did so want us to be friends."

"Yeah. Me, too."

"And we got on so well together yesterday."

"That's what I thought." He remembered the howling dervish who had attacked him. "Now I see why you spent so much time talking about Donna."

"Forget her," said Tania.

"How can I? She's my sister."

"Forget her as far as I'm concerned."

Tania eased him back down on to the wall again and sat beside him. Stuart was slowly rallying. Other pupils were still drifting past and he was collecting some very envious glances. His pain gradually began to ease.

"Would you like to take me out again?" she said.

"Well . . ."

"We won't even mention Donna this time."

"Promise?"

"We'll just talk about us."

"Will we?" His resistance was crumbling.

"How about tonight?"

"Yes, yes. Fine."

"Where would you like to go?"

"Don't mind. You choose, Tania."

"What about the Odeon? That new horror film."

Stuart's mind whirred. He had been promoted. Taking her out to a coffee bar was one thing but going to the cinema with her was quite another. Sitting in the dark with Tania Hancox opened up all sorts of possibilities and the fact that it was a horror film meant that she might well need to be comforted. It was an enticing prospect. Not so enticing was the prospect of Donna's reaction. This would be another betrayal of her even if they never talked about her.

Remorse fought with romance. Tania nudged him.

"Is it on?"

"Yes," he said. "It's on."

By the time she got to the hotel, the whole incident had been put behind her. Donna Melrose was nothing if not resilient. Having vented her fury on her brother, she felt much better and she was far too sensible to let anything that Tania Hancox did rile her for too long. It was now dead and buried. Besides, she had a wonderful treat in store. An exclusive interview with

Emilie Deltchev. Nothing could take the lustre off that.

As she went up in the lift, her mouth was dry and her heart was pounding. She tried to rehearse the questions that she wanted to ask but they would not come out in the right order. She was still wrestling with the problem when the lift stopped to let her out.

Donna walked along the corridor until she came to the right room then she made a big effort to compose herself. While she was still trying to fill her lungs, the door opened and the eagle eyes of the redoubtable Terezie Klimenko studied her. Donna squirmed under the scrutiny.

"Miss Melrose?"

"Yes."

"Ten minutes."

"I know."

"Come in."

Emilie was sitting on the bed with her knees up. She hopped off and came to shake Donna's hand. It was a warm welcome and the young reporter drew a lot of strength from it. Terezie waved them to chairs then sat between them. It was obvious that she was going to be much more than an interpreter. She was there as a censor. There were certain questions that would just not be allowed.

The woman gave a curt nod.

"Begin."

"Thank you." Donna had her pad and pencil ready. "Um . . . did you always want to be a gymnast, Emilie?"

Terezie translated and they were away.

Despite the restraints, the interview went quite

well. Emilie was very frank. She answered all the questions without hesitation and Donna was encouraged to press her on one or two personal matters. It was at this point that Terezie used her veto. She just shook her head and the questions went untranslated. When the woman flicked an eye at the bedside clock, Donna knew that her time was almost up. She put her final question.

"What do you think of England?"

Emilie did not wait for any interpreter.

"I love your country . . ."

Terezie looked at her sharply but her attention was immediately distracted by a noise from the bathroom. She got up and went to investigate. The girls watched her go in through the door then they heard a dull thud. Donna stood up in alarm but Emilie's face brightened.

Two men then came surging in from the bathroom. Both were young, agile and determined. Donna was given no time to protest as one of them grabbed her unceremoniously and held a large pad over her mouth and nose. As soon as she inhaled the chloroform, her struggles ceased and she began to drift off into unconsciousness. She caught a glimpse of Emilie being overpowered in the same way then her knees sagged. The last thing she saw was the ceiling of the room swirling wildly away from her.

Then came oblivion.

Chapter 4

Terezie Klimenko took a long time to recover. When her eyes finally opened, she saw that she was lying on the floor of the bathroom. As her head slowly cleared, she began to remember what had happened. Two men attacked her. One of them held a pad over her mouth and nostrils. She could still smell the pungent odour. Terezie was galvanised into action. Leaping up from the floor, she ran into the bedroom to find it empty. She raced out in a panic, darted along the corridor then pounded on a door.

"Viktor! Quick – open up!"

"Coming!" he shouted.

"Hurry! Hurry!"

The door opened and she almost fell into his arms.

"What's the matter?" he said.

"Emilie. They've taken her."

"Who?"

"Two men. She's been kidnapped."

Viktor did not wait for an explanation. His response was immediate. He snatched up the telephone, asked for the manager and told him what had happened. A security alert came into operation at once. Every exit was sealed off and the hotel security staff went up to the tenth floor to get more details and to begin a thorough search. The police were summoned instantly. The hotel buzzed with activity.

But they were too late. Minutes before Terezie had

regained consciousness, two men in white coats loaded a large wicker basket into a transit van that was parked outside the service entrance. As the vehicle pulled away, the name ACME LAUNDRY could be seen on its side.

It was soon swallowed up by traffic.

Stuart Melrose could not understand why he was not enjoying it all much more. Sitting beside Tania Hancox in the back row of the Odeon cinema, he looked vacantly up at the screen without seeing anything of the film. The other boys would have been insanely jealous if they knew where he was and with whom but the gloss had somehow gone off the occasion for him. He was as eager as before to take Tania out but he realised they were not alone together. Someone else had come along with them.

Donna. His sister.

He knew that she would hate him for sneaking off with Tania again but he could not help himself. His only hope was that she would not find out. He had no wish to rouse Donna's ire any further. She was frightening when she got into a rage. Besides, he did not want to hurt her any more. She had really suffered at Tania's hands and he was indirectly responsible. He kicked himself for talking about Donna in such an unguarded way. He would be much more careful in future.

Tania Hancox nestled up against him.

"What's wrong?" she hissed.

"Nothing."

"You did want to see this film, didn't you?"

"Sure."

"With me, I mean."

"Yeah."

"Then why freeze up on me?"

"Eh?"

"Do something, Stuart."

"What do you mean?"

"We're supposed to be together."

"We are, Tania."

"Then show it. Put your arm around me."

"Ah. Right . . ."

Stuart had fantasized many times about the moment when he could do just that. Now that it had at last arrived, it had none of the pleasure he expected. Instead of slipping his arm gently around her so that he could bring her closer to him, he sat bolt upright and let the palm of his hand rest against the back of her neck.

Tania Hancox clicked her tongue.

"You can do better than that."

"Can I?"

"Come here, silly."

She pulled his arm right around her then rested her head on his shoulder. He could smell the lacquer on her hair as it mingled with the aroma of her perfume. At any other time, he would have been deliriously happy but his guilt still stirred.

"Great film, isn't it?" she said.

"Terrific."

"Squeeze me hard during the creepy bits."

"I will."

"And relax. We came out to have fun."

"Yeah. I know."

But Stuart remained tense and uncomfortable. He

tried to remind himself that nobody could see them in the dark and that his sister would never know that they had spent another evening together but all his reassurances failed. He was having a wonderful time with a girl whom he adored but he was also aware that he was committing a sort of crime.

When he looked at the screen again, he was jolted.

All he could see on it was Donna.

When she finally came out of her long sleep, she had no idea where she was. She seemed to be curled up inside some kind of box, lying on a pile of sheets. Her limbs were cramped and her head was aching. As she felt around inside her little prison, she touched something that made her go cold all over.

It was a body.

There was someone else in there.

Donna stifled a scream. The body had felt stiff and lifeless. They had locked her in there with a corpse. All of a sudden she wanted to be sick and started to retch. Then a faint sigh came from her companion and her legs moved slightly. Donna was at once relieved and terrified. Where was she and who was this stranger lying beside her?

It was only when her brain started to function again that she had a vague memory of the assault at the hotel. She and Emilie had been set upon by the two men. They must have been smuggled out somehow. Donna could tell from the noise and the vibrations that they were now travelling in some kind of vehicle. Sounds of traffic occasionally filtered through.

Where were they going?

And why?

All of the possibilities were alarming. She went numb as she recalled some of the dreadful stories she had read in the newspapers about young girls being abducted. Even as she feared for herself, however, she had an uprush of sympathy for Emilie. It must be far worse for her. She was in a foreign country. And she knew so little about the dangers of the real world. Having been cloistered for so long in her gymnastic career, she was totally unfitted to cope with this sort of emergency.

Donna Melrose was not sure that she herself could handle the situation but she would try her best. As the Czechoslovakian girl began to stir, Donna called up all her courage and determination.

The basket creaked as Emilie tried to sit up.

"Terezie? Terezie?" she whimpered.

"Don't be afraid," said Donna.

The other girl started at the sound of her voice.

"Kdo je tam?"

"It's me. Your friend."

"Kdo?"

"Donna Melrose."

Emilie was trembling with fear. Her trip to England had been so rich with promise and it had now turned into a nightmare. She was consumed by a sense of dread.

Donna reached out to pull her close.

"Don't worry, Emilie. I'll look after you."

The two men in the lift wondered what all the commotion was about. They had heard voices raised and footsteps charging along corridors. It was the last thing they wanted. They needed the hotel to be a place of ordered calm before they could go about their business.

The lift stopped on the top floor. After checking that the corridor was empty, the man with the horn-rimmed glasses led the way to the emergency exit. Opening it soundlessly, he went swiftly through it and up a steel staircase that led to the roof of the building. His accomplice followed him, carrying a black briefcase and looking like a businessman on his way to a conference.

They crouched behind a water tank.

"This is it, old chap."

"Ready when you are."

"Get the rope out."

"It's right here."

The young man opened the briefcase but he did not get the chance to take out any of the equipment he had brought. Down below in the street, they heard the telltale whine of police cars approaching at speed. They ran to the parapet and peered over. Three police cars were screeching to a halt at the front entrance of the hotel. A fourth was haring around to the rear.

The man in the spectacles was furious.

"Blast!"

"What's up?"

"Mission aborted."

"All off?"

"For the time being."

"What do we do?"

"Get out of here fast!"

"Let's go!"

Cliff Melrose was still at Hillcrest when the telephone

rang in his office. The anguished voice of his wife came on the line.

"Is that you, Cliff?"

"Yeah. What's up?"

"Something terrible's happened!"

"Eh?"

"The police have just rung."

"Why?"

"It's Donna . . ."

Cliff could hear the tears in her voice. He got to his feet in anxiety and his heart constricted.

"An accident?"

"Nothing like that."

"Then what, Maggie?"

"She went to inverview that girl."

"Emilie Deltchev. I know. I set it up."

"They've disappeared, Cliff."

"Who?"

"Donna and Emilie. They've been kidnapped."

"When? How?"

"The details are all a bit hazy."

"Are they sure about this?"

"They want you there as soon as possible."

"What about you?"

"There's a police car coming for me."

"I'll see you there."

He put down the receiver and gave himself a few seconds to take it all in. Then he went out of his office and sprinted all the way down the main staircase. One thought kept worming its way through his mind.

What had they done to Donna?

Locked inside the laundry basket, Donna and Emilie

held hands to comfort each other. They had tried to raise the lid of their prison but it was held shut by thick straps. Both of them had conquered their initial feeling of horror and they no longer lay there fearing the worst. They made an effort to come to terms with the situation.

Emilie spoke in halting English.

"Where we . . . are?"

"I wish I knew."

"Why . . . they take?"

"I'm not sure. But they wanted us badly."

"Pardon?"

"It was obviously well-organised," said Donna. "They knew where your room was and how to get into it. And they had their escape all planned as well."

"No . . . understand."

"Sorry, Emilie."

"Speak slow. My English . . . poor."

"It's better than my Czech!"

Donna gave a hollow laugh then tensed as she felt the vehicle slow. They seemed to be rolling over an uneven surface. When the van came to a sudden halt, they were thrown against each other. Someone got out of the cab then they heard the sound of a metal door being lifted up. The van rolled forward before stopping again and the metal door clanged back into position.

Heavy feet approached then the rear doors of the vehicle were opened. Someone clambered into the back and started to undo the leather straps. Donna and Emilie instinctively tightened their grip on each other. The lid was thrown back and light flooded in from a naked electric bulb. They shielded their eyes for a moment. When they were able to look at their captors, they saw the two men who had abducted them. One had a beard and the other had a livid scar across his chin.

The bearded man gave them a welcoming smile. "Dobry vecer!"

"What do you want with us?" said Donna firmly.

He blinked in astonishment and turned to Emilie.

"Kdo je tato mlada pani?"

"Donna," she said. "Moje pritelkyne."

The two men traded a look of undisguised anger then the one with the beard stared coldly at Donna. When he spoke, his voice had a heavy accent.

"We wanted Emilie and Zuzana. Not you." His eyes narrowed to pinpricks. "We don't need an English girl. You're no use to us at all."

Donna was in an even worse predicament now.

They had kidnapped her by mistake.

"There must be something more you can tell us," insisted Cliff Melrose. "Our daughter's life might be at stake."

"We appreciate that, sir," said the detective.

"Don't you have any idea what happened?"

"Bear with us, Mr Melrose."

"Why take Donna?" said Maggie anxiously. "That's what we can't understand."

"Nor can we at this stage."

"Have the kidnappers been in touch?" asked Cliff.

"Not as yet, sir."

"Let me speak to them when they do," he said with sudden belligerence. "Just wait till I get my hands on them – whoever they bloody well are!"

"Leave this to us, Mr Melrose."

Detective-Superintendent Jackson was a big, sturdy man with a broken nose he had collected somewhere in the line of duty. He had deployed his men around the hotel and taken on the difficult tasks of calming the outraged Czechoslovakian manager and giving what reassurance he could to Cliff and Maggie. They were now in the hotel office that had been put at their disposal.

The phone rang and Jackson picked it up. He got a message, grunted into the receiver then put it back down.

"You'll have to excuse me," he said.

"Any new information?" pressed Cliff.

"None, I'm afraid."

"Isn't there something we can do?" said Maggie.

"Stay here, Mrs Melrose. I'll have tea sent in."

There was a tap on the door and it was opened by a tall, well-dressed man in his thirties. He had an air of authority about him that made the much older detective instantly deferential. The newcomer threw a glance at the anguished parents then nodded for Superintendent Jackson to follow him out. The door closed behind them.

Maggie turned to her husband in alarm.

"Who was that?"

"Special Branch."

"How do you know?"

"You can tell."

"Why are Special Branch involved?"

"Because it's not just a kidnapping."

"I'm not with you, Cliff."

"It's political."

The forensic team did a thorough job in Emilie's room under the scrutiny of Terezie Klimenko. She watched them take photographs, fingerprints, even strands of hair from the carpet. She was also on hand when a detective lifted up the pillow on Emilie's bed and found a book stuffed down the back of the mattress. He pulled it out carefully and looked at its front cover with a puzzled frown.

He held it out to Terezie.

"She wanted to keep this hidden for some reason."

"What is it?"

"You tell me. It's in Czech."

Terezie took the book and examined it. Her jaw tightened and there was a flash of annoyance in her eyes.

"Well?" asked the detective.

"It is nothing," she said dismissively.

"Translate that title for me."

Terezie stared at the book with evident distaste.

"Colloquial English."

The room was small, bare and low-ceilinged. They were upstairs in what seemed to be an old farmhouse. When they peered through the window, they could see nothing but the ghostly outline of trees swaying rhythmically in the wind. It was eerie. Donna consulted her watch. It was almost exactly two hours since she first arrived at the hotel. They had been jumped on some ten minutes later. Allowing time for their journey from Emilie's room to the back of the van, they could still have been on the road for well over an hour and a half. The vehicle had been travelling at speed. They could be a long way from London now. It all added to her sense of bewilderment.

They had the consolation of being together.

"Don't be frightened, Emilie."

"I no like."

"Everything will work out okay."

"I cold . . . unhappy."

"Me, too. But we must keep up our spirits."

"Spirits?" The word was not in her vocabulary.

Donna went to sit on the floor beside her.

"We can face anything together."

"We friends."

"Yes," said Donna. "Good friends."

They had been put in the room while the two men worked out their next move. Donna grasped at a few straws of comfort. They were not tied up and they had not been roughly handled. Their captors had been almost courteous with Emilie, well aware of her fame and full of a kind of grudging respect for her. They had been more curt with Donna but she had not been threatened in any way.

She gave Emilie a smile of encouragement. Dreadful as her ordeal was, she was at least sharing it with the person she admired most in the world. All that she had expected was ten minutes with Emilie Deltchev. Instead of that, she was now being held in captivity with the girl and adversity was drawing them closer together. Emilie was scared but, like Donna, she had a fighting spirit. Neither girl would give up easily.

"What did they say?" asked Donna.

"Say?"

"Those men. Talking in Czech."

"They want Zuzana."

"Why?"

"Zuzana and me . . . you wrong."

"I gathered that."

"They talk . . . about Prague."

"And?"

"That's all."

"Prague?" Donna scratched her head. "Do you think they want to take you back to Czechoslovakia?"

Emilie shivered at the suggestion and tears welled up in her eyes. Donna put a protective arm around her.

"What's the matter, Emilie?"

"No tell . . ."

"Don't you want to go back home?"

Emilie did not get the chance to reply. Someone came bounding up the stairs outside and inserted a key in the lock. Donna got to her feet and stood in front of the little gymnast to defend her. Her bravery faltered when the door swung open.

The bearded man was pointing a gun at her.

"You!" he snarled. "Come with me!"

Donna feared for her life.

Chapter 5

Eventually, it got the better of him. The combination of darkness, horror and Tania Hancox proved lethal. Stuart Melrose succumbed. He still had twinges of conscience but they became less frequent. When he started to watch the film, he found it very entertaining and ideal for his purposes. Each twist in the story was more gruesome than the last and it brought squeals of fright from Tania. He had almost unlimited licence to pull her close and give her soothing little kisses. Both of them were sorry when the film finally came to a close with the agonizing death of the monster who had terrorized a whole city.

They came out into the fresh air.

"Smashing film!" said Stuart.

"Thanks for taking me."

"Pleasure. Uh, Tania . . ."

"Yeah."

"Can I ask you a favour?"

"Of course."

"Don't say anything about this to Donna, will you?"

"Not a syllable," she promised. "I don't want to make things difficult for you at home, Stuart. We'll keep this a secret between us. Okay?"

A load was suddenly lifted from his mind and he squeezed her hand in gratitude. Donna could not be harmed by something she knew nothing about. It let him off the hook. He could be friends with Tania without upsetting his sister. The best of both worlds.

Stuart exploited his new-found confidence.

"Where will I take you next time?"

"Wherever you like."

"What I like is being alone with you."

"Suits me."

"Just name the day."

"How are you fixed at the weekend?"

"It's pretty free."

"Sunday night, then."

"Sunday?"

"Come round to my place."

"Won't your parents mind?"

"They won't even know," she said airily. "They go out every Sunday. We'll have the house all to ourselves."

Stuart could not believe his luck. In the space of forty-eight hours, his relationship with Tania Hancox had improved in leaps and bounds. Until the day before, he had been just one of many hopeful suitors who watched her longingly from afar. He had now taken her out twice and was effectively her boyfriend. It was intoxicating.

His sister vanished from his mind altogether. With a proprietary arm around Tania's shoulders, he walked along the main street. Stuart had taken other girls out but none could compete with Tania Hancox. He loved her. In two short days, he moved from intense admiration of her to complete infatuation.

He was tempted yet again to lower his guard.

Tania saw Hillcrest looming up ahead of them.

"Do you think he can make it work?"

"Who?"

"Your father."

"Dad? Oh, yes. He's got amazing drive. If anyone can make a success of Hillcrest, it's him."

"He was a footballer, wasn't he?"

"Yes. A striker. Eight years with Arsenal."

"Did he ever play for England?"

"Lots of times. Then he had a bad injury. Cartilege trouble. He had three operations but he was never the same player. So he retired early."

"What did he do then?"

"Joined the coaching staff. Dad's a great motivator. He knows how to lift people up. Of course, the next step was management and that meant starting in the Fourth Division. We had to live in Scunthorpe for a year!"

"Sounds awful."

"It wasn't too bad. Luckily, Dad got an offer from Leicester City. Assistant manager. After a couple of years, they sacked the manager and Dad took over. Got them back into the First Division."

"Then what happened?"

"He came here."

Stuart glossed over the fact that his father had been forced to resign from the club and had been out of work for some while. He was very proud of his father's sporting achievements and he played down the inevitable setbacks that Cliff had suffered.

Tania glanced up at Hillcrest as they went past.

"What are his plans for this place?"

"Oh, Dad's very ambitious."

"In what way?"

Encouraged by her interest, he talked freely about

the ideas that his father had for turning Hillcrest into a profitable enterprise. Tania lapped it up, seeing the chance of further rewards from her uncle. Stuart was well into his stride when he saw something up ahead that stopped him in mid-sentence.

Two familiar figures were coming out of the Regent Hotel with a uniformed officer at their heels. It was his parents. Even from thirty yards away, he could see how tired and dejected they were. They got into a police car and were driven quickly away.

Stuart was rocked to the core.

Emilie Deltchev took the mug of coffee from him and eyed him suspiciously. She was grateful to have something warm between her hands and the drink revived her when she sipped it, but she did not trust the man at all. Even though he was making an effort to be friendly, she did not relax. The man with the scar on his chin crouched down in front of her and experimented with a smile. She shrunk even further away from him.

He spoke to her quietly in Czech.

"I'm sorry to have to do this, Emilie. It's not personal. We have nothing against you."

"Then let me go," she said.

"I'm afraid we can't."

"Why did you kidnap me?"

"It's best if you don't know that."

"What about Donna?"

"Forget about her."

"She's my friend. Don't hurt her."

"The English girl has nothing to do with this." He

leant in a little closer. "What we need from you is a little cooperation."

"No!" she retorted.

"It's in your own interests."

"I'll do nothing to help."

"Don't be stupid, Emilie."

"I hate you."

"We've treated you well so far."

"You dragged us away from the hotel," she said indignantly. "You locked us in that terrible basket. Is that what you call treating us well?"

"Calm down," he warned.

"They'll catch you."

"Shut up."

"They'll punish you."

"Do as you're told!"

"I hope they lock you away for ever!"

When he reached forward to restrain her, she threw the coffee in his face and made him reel back. He cursed loudly and wiped himself dry with his sleeve. Emilie was torn between fear and defiance. The man looked at her through narrowed lids.

"That was a very stupid thing to do."

"Then let us out of here."

"No chance."

"Why not?"

"There's too much at stake."

"At least, let Donna go," she reasoned. "You don't need her. I'm the one you want. Let Donna out."

"Is she a good friend of yours?" he said.

"Yes."

"Then you don't want any harm to come to her."

"Of course not."

"So – you do as we tell you."

"No."

"Say goodbye to your friend, then."

He turned on his heel and opened the door.

"Wait!" she cried.

He paused. "Well?"

"Please don't hurt her."

Having found the way to put pressure on Emilie, the man did so without compunction.

"Help us or you never see her alive again."

Emilie nodded in defeat and lowered her head.

"I knew you'd see sense in the end," he said.

Her voice took on a pleading note as she looked up.

"Why are you doing all this?"

"For Czechoslovakia."

Donna Melrose was in an equally unpleasant situation. She was seated on an upright chair in the living room being interrogated by the bearded man. The gun was now in his belt as he stood over her. When they heard the yell from upstairs, they glanced up in unison at the ceiling. Donna guessed rightly that Emilie was showing resistance. It steeled her in her own emergency.

The man sat down and fired his questions at her.

"Let's go through it once more."

"I've told you the truth."

"I want to be sure. What is your name?"

"Donna Melrose."

"Why were you in Emilie's room?"

"I was interviewing her."

"For what?"

"The school newspaper."

"Newspaper? In a school?"

"Mrs Inigo started it," explained Donna. "She's our English teacher. We submit articles by Friday and they get printed in the next week's edition."

"And they let you speak with Emilie Deltchev?"

"Only because of my father."

"Ah, yes. The Director of Hillcrest."

"He'll come looking for you."

"They will not find us here."

"You can't keep us locked up for ever."

"A few days is all we need."

"But Emilie is competing on Saturday."

"I don't think so."

"She must!" exclaimed Donna, jumping to her feet. "Everyone is coming to see her. You don't know what this means to Hillcrest. If you don't let Emilie . . ."

Her voice tailed away as the gun was pulled out.

The other man came into the room and the accomplices talked volubly in Czech. Donna could not understand the words but the gestures were graphic and gave her some clue what they were talking about. She also learned the names of the two men. The one with the beard was called Pavel and the other was Lazlo. After a long conversation, they turned back to her.

Pavel pointed a finger and gave a command. Lazlo produced a length of rope from his pocket and moved towards her. Donna backed away until she came up against the dank stone wall.

"What are you going to do?" she asked.

"Put you somewhere safe," said Pavel.

"Let me go back to Emilie."

"I give the orders."

Donna made a sudden rush for the door but Lazlo was too quick for her. He got her hands behind her back and started to tie them together. Donna screamed hard.

Pavel glowered threateningly at her.

"Would you like another sniff of chloroform?"

Donna subsided. She was powerless.

A home which was usually so lively and full of laughter was now as quiet as a graveyard. The Melrose family sat in the kitchen in grim silence. Cliff stared blankly ahead, Stuart rubbed his hands nervously together and Maggie was motionless with her eyes closed against the ordeal of the wait. Even Wilf, who could normally be relied upon to cough or belch or rid himself of another grumble, was cowed. Donna had been forcibly taken away. The sheer horror of it weighed down on them.

It was Stuart who broke through the gloom.

"Maybe they'll let Donna go," he said brightly.

"If only they would!" sighed Maggie.

"It's not as if they need her," he said, trying to think it through. "If the Special Branch are in on it, then it must be political. Nothing to do with Donna at all. She just got caught up in it. They'll let her go."

"They can't, son," said Cliff.

"Why not?"

"Because Donna's seen them. She can identify them."

"I hadn't thought of that."

"They have. That's why she's in such danger."

Stuart gulped as he considered the implications.

"Because they don't need her, they might . . ."

Maggie got up purposefully and went to the sink.

"Anyone for tea?" she said, filling the kettle under the tap. "No more of that kind of talk, Stuart, please. We have worries enough without you stoking them up."

"Sorry, Mum."

"All we can do is to wait. And pray."

"Praying never does any good," murmured Wilf. "Only thing it ever gave me was arthritis in my knees."

They lapsed into another silence. It was shattered by the ringing of the telephone. Cliff bounded into the hall to answer it, hoping for good news. The others went after him and watched.

"Hello," he said. "Cliff Melrose." His body sagged with disappointment. "Oh, it's you, Kim . . . No, there's been no developments. Just what you saw on News at Ten. It's all we know ourselves . . . Yes, I will . . . thanks, Kim. Good of you to ring . . . Cheerio."

He put the receiver down and looked at them.

"Kim. Sends all her love. Thinking of us."

"That's kind," said Maggie.

"At least, it wasn't one of them bleeding reporters again," said Wilf, shuffling back into the kitchen. "How many have rung us up so far. Ten? Fifteen? Pests! That's what they are. Never know when to leave you alone. All they want is their flipping story!"

Maggie followed him and plugged in the kettle. Cliff and Stuart stayed in the hall. The boy had never seen his father look so distraught.

"Anything I can do, Dad?"

"Sweat it out like the rest of us."

"Donna's as tough as they come. She'll be okay."

"Against two men as desperate as that?" said Cliff. "They used chloroform against Terezie Klimenko. They obviously meant business."

"But how did they get into that bathroom?"

"Through the window, the police reckon. There's a balcony outside. They probably got access to it from the room above. Who knows? The simple fact is that it was well-planned and well-executed."

"Looks like it."

"They probably had the Czech team under surveillance from the moment they arrived. First thing tomorrow, I'll speak to my staff."

"Why?"

"To ask if any of them saw anyone hanging around when Emilie was in the building. We had lots of autograph hunters trying to sneak in to see her. Those two men might have got into Hillcrest somehow."

Stuart was not listening. An image had just popped into his mind. An image of a well-dressed man in a pair of hornrimmed glasses, finding his way into the balcony of the sports hall and pretending he was looking for the bar. Stuart was convinced that he was involved somehow.

But what was he to do? If he told his father, he would be confessing that he had brought Tania Hancox into Hillcrest against Cliff's express wishes. There would be a horrendous row. Stuart did not want that, especially at a time when nerves were so fraught.

Another thought troubled him. It burned into his brain like hot iron. If he had been more alert at the time and reported the man's presence, then the Czech visitors might have been warned in advance that their star gymnast was under threat.

More to the point, Donna might have been saved.

Stuart shuddered at his own shortcomings.

He was to blame.

Councillor Harry Wyman drove home in his black Rover with a grin of triumph. A five-minute chat with his niece had given him some more invaluable information to use against Cliff Melrose and he had shown his gratitude to Tania with a flourish of his wallet. His pleasure was checked for a few minutes when he heard the news of the kidnap on the car radio. He was naturally concerned about the safety of the two girls but their disappearance could be advantageous to him. By the time he turned into his drive, the grin was back in place and broader than ever.

Inside his house, he went straight to the telephone. The number that he dialled rang out for some time before he got an answer. A crisp voice came on the line.

"Who is it?"

"Mr Griefer?"

"Yes."

"Harry Wyman."

"It's late, Harry. I hope this is not a social call. I haven't any time for idle chatter."

"I've got a present for you, Mr Griefer."

"What kind of present?"

"Haven't you heard the news?"

"No, Harry."

"Emilie Deltchev has been kidnapped."

"Who on earth is she when she's at home?"

"The Olympic gymnastic champion," said Harry, barely able to contain his glee. "She was due to perform at Hillcrest as part of the Czechoslovakian team."

"Why should this interest me?" said Griefer.

"Because the whole event will probably have to be cancelled now. At an enormous cost. Don't you catch my drift? This could be a catastrophe for Cliff Melrose."

There was a complacent chuckle from Griefer.

"That is good news, Harry. Thank you."

"There's more to come. I've got some dope on Melrose that'll make him squirm."

"Excellent."

"Is your consortium still keen to buy Hillcrest?"

"Very keen."

"Then get your cheque book ready."

"Don't count your chickens, Harry."

"Oh, I've got him this time," said the other with flabby delight. "I've got the lever to get him out of that job for good. Stand by, Mr Griefer. I'm going to hand Hillcrest to you on a plate."

"We'll honour our side of the deal."

"I get my percentage?"

"After you deliver."

"Oh, I will. No doubt about that. Give me a week and it'll be over. Cliff Melrose will be finished."

"And we move in."

It was cold, damp and miserable in the larder and only a small shaft of light came in under the door. Donna Melrose was almost in despair. Her hands were tied behind her back and she was locked in. She did not dare to rest against the wall because it was covered in flaking whitewash. Afraid of spiders, she was even more alarmed by the scratching noises in the far corner.

Mice or rats? It was unsettling.

She tried to take her mind off her own worries by concentrating on Emilie. The girl must be in a state of torment. Evidently, she was being held for ransom. But by whom? And to what end? It seemed so cruel and unnecessary to use someone as innocent and harmless as Emilie in this way. She was a pawn in some kind of dangerous game.

What would happen to her if the two men lost?

Her ears picked up the sound of a radio. It was too far away for her to hear it clearly but she collected an important scrap of information.

The BBC announcer intoned the news solemnly.

"Police believe they made their escape in a laundry van. There have been unconfirmed sightings of it on the westbound carriageway of the M4. Police are appealing to anyone who has seen a white transit van belonging to the Acme Laundry Company. The number to ring is . . ."

The radio was switched off angrily and she could hear the two men locked in angry debate. Donna Melrose was prompted into action. Pressing herself backwards, she lifted her leg high so that her foot reached the opposite wall. She began to scrape off the whitewash.

Donna was writing something.

Chapter 6

Kingsmead was buzzing with speculation next morning. The abduction of Emilie Deltchev was a major news item that had flashed around the whole world but it was the kidnap of Donna Melrose which preoccupied her fellow-pupils. It brought the school itself a lot of publicity. Journalists descended on Kingsmead in droves and there was even a television crew outside the main gate to get some footage of the children as they arrived. Donna's classmates were eagerly sought out for comment and several who had never really liked her now claimed that they were close friends and talked freely about her to the press. The headmaster gave a televised interview and Jane Ryder was brought in to talk about Donna's gymnastic prowess. Kingsmead was famous for a while. It rubbed off on everyone.

Stuart Melrose had been wisely kept away from school that day. There was no way he could have escaped being hounded by journalists and mobbed by the other pupils. And it would have been impossible for him to concentrate on any of his lessons. Besides, he wanted to be with his family to lend moral support and to be on hand when there were any new developments.

He was missed by one person in particular.

"Have you heard anything?" asked Tania Hancox.

"No," said Kim Davison.

"Come on, you can tell me."

"You're the last person I'd tell."

"Have you spoken to Donna's family?"

"What if I have?"

"They must have said something."

"They did, Tania."

"Well?"

"Mind your own business!"

The two girls were walking into the school hall for morning assembly. Tania Hancox had been secretly pleased when she had first heard the news about Donna's kidnap but that pleasure was now tinged with envy. The incident was splashed across every newspaper. It was the lead item in every news bulletin. Everyone was talking about it. The name of Donna Melrose had been turned by the media into a household word. Tania Hancox was jealous. Her arch enemy might be in danger but she was also taking part in a strange adventure. It was more exciting than another dreary day at Kingsmead.

"Serves her right!" she decided.

"Who?"

"Donna Melrose. Boasting about that exclusive she was going to get with Emilie Deltchev."

"She didn't boast," said Kim. "She's not like you."

"This'll take her down a peg or two."

"Don't be such a cow!"

"She's been getting above herself."

"You just can't take it, can you?"

"What?"

"Donna getting all this attention."

"Couldn't care two hoots."

"Yes, you could," said Kim. "That's why you tried

to get something out of me. Because you think I might know something that you don't. You're just jealous."

"No, I'm not."

"Nasty, jealous and resentful."

"Shut your face, Kim Davison!" stormed Tania. "If I want to know the latest, I don't have to come to you. I can get it straight from Stuart."

"Since when?"

"Since he started taking me out. I've got him eating out of my hand. Stuart would tell me anything."

Tania flounced off to sit with her friends.

Kim Davison was stung to the quick.

Cliff Melrose did not believe that things could get worse until he went to work that morning. Viktor Zaremba was waiting outside his office with a tight jaw and blazing eyes. Cliff conducted him in and waved him to a seat.

"I will stand," said Viktor pointedly.

"Tea? Coffee?"

"I will not be staying long."

"I can't tell you how sorry I am about all this," said Cliff. "It's a tragedy."

"Emilie is the greatest gymnast in the world."

"I know that, Mr Zaremba."

"This is more than a tragedy," said Viktor. "It is a national disaster for Czechoslovakia."

"I appreciate that."

"We hold you partly responsible."

"Me?"

"You were in charge of security."

"Not at the hotel," reminded Cliff. "That was agreed when we drew up the contract. I was to handle everything at Hillcrest but not outside this building. It's just not my province."

"Maybe it should have been, Mr Melrose."

"In what way?"

"If you'd done your job properly, Emilie Deltchev would not have been kidnapped."

"Hey, now hang on a minute," said Cliff. "She's not the only one they took from the Regency Hotel. My own daughter was abducted as well. I know this has been a terrible blow for you but I'm going through hell myself."

Viktor Zaremba stood to attention and nodded his apology. He was fighting to control his emotions. Like Cliff, he had obviously had very little sleep during the night. Both of them were haggard and exhausted.

"It is all very regrettable," said Viktor.

"That's an understatement!"

"We have no alternative, Mr Melrose."

"I don't follow."

"Cancel the event."

"Cancel it!"

"There is no way we can compete."

"But you must."

"Without Emilie? It is unthinkable."

"But everything has been set up," pleaded Cliff. "All the tickets have been sold and I've hired extra catering staff. If you pull out now, months of hard work will be thrown down the drain."

"That cannot be helped."

"It can. Fulfil your contract."

"Not without Emilie."

"She wouldn't want it ruined because of her. Think of Emilie. Do it for her sake."

"We have considered that, believe me," said Viktor. "But it is not so easy. The other girls have lost heart. They would not do justice to themselves in this contest and I will not have them letting Czechoslovakia down."

Cliff did all he could to persuade the manager but Viktor was adamant. The team had to withdraw and the whole event had to be scrapped. As a last resort, Cliff offered a compromise.

"Don't make any public announcement."

"How do you mean?"

"Let everyone think it's going ahead."

"But it's not, Mr Melrose."

"What if Emilie was rescued?"

"That would change everything."

"You'd be prepared to compete?"

"Possibly but there is no likelihood of that."

"Don't rule out the efficiency of our police and Special Branch," said Cliff. "They'll track her down somehow. I know. You'll get Emilie back."

"Safe and sound?"

"If those men wanted to harm her, they could have done that at the hotel. They wouldn't go to all that trouble unless she was highly valuable to them. My guess is they'll be making a ransom demand at any moment."

"That is what the police believe."

"Let's leave them to get on with their job. Our major concern is tomorrow's event. I'd like to come to an agreement with you, Mr Zaremba."

"I'm listening."

"If we cancel, it will knock Hillcrest for six. A lot

of time and money has gone into this project and we can't afford to throw it all away."

"No Emilie, no competition."

"I was coming to that," said Cliff. "If you promise to hold your horses until tomorrow, I'll undertake to get your world champion back again."

"How?"

"I don't know but I'll find a way somehow."

"If only I could believe that."

"Don't withdraw yet. Please."

"Well . . . "

"Delay your decision. That's all I ask."

Viktor thought it over. Cliff waited anxiously.

"All right," said the manager.

"Thank you! This means so much to me."

"Twenty-four hours."

"We'll do it."

They shook hands then Viktor went out. Cliff flopped into the seat behind his desk with his head in his hands. The threat of cancellation had brought him out into a cold sweat. It was the worst possible thing that could happen to Hillcrest at such a difficult time and it would deliver him up to his enemies bound and gagged.

Relief was fractured by anxiety. He had vowed to get Emilie Deltchev back but how? And what about Donna? Both had vanished without trace. He himself did not have the resources to search for them. It was hopeless.

A wave of despair washed over him but he was not drowned. A lifebelt was thrown to him in the form of a telephone call. He snatched up the receiver.

"Hillcrest."

"Mr Melrose?"

"Yes."

"Superintendent Jackson."

"Any news?"

"The kidnappers have made contact with the Czech Embassy. They're demanding the release of six political prisoners back home in Prague."

"How do we know it's not a hoax call."

"Emilie Deltchev spoke herself."

"What about Donna?" asked Cliff urgently. "Was there any mention of my daughter."

"I'm afraid not, sir. But I can tell you one hopeful piece of information."

"Well?"

"This is strictly confidential, mind you."

"Of course, Superintendent."

"We had some calls in about that transit van. It's enabled us to pinpoint its whereabouts fairly accurately. Our chaps are moving in right now. Keep your fingers crossed, Mr Melrose. We could be in luck."

"Thank God!" said Cliff.

The police helicopter swooped low over the farmhouse. It looked deserted. They radioed their position then hovered overhead. As soon as the pilot saw the police cars converging on the farm, he brought the helicopter down in an adjacent field. Six armed detectives leapt out and ran beneath the whirring rotor blades. Other men spilled out of the cars and the place was soon surrounded.

After studying the house through binoculars, the senior officer decided that it was safe to approach. He gave the signal and his men closed in. The first thing to be found was the transit van, still in the garage with its half-empty laundry basket. Detectives swarmed over it for clues. Others, meanwhile, had gained access to the house itself and they soon established that it was empty. Signs of a hasty departure were everywhere.

One of the men hailed the senior officer.

"Over here, Commander."

"Where?"

"In the larder."

"What have you got?"

"A helping hand, by the look of it."

Crossing to the larder, the Commander saw what his man had found. Written in the fading whitewash on the wall were two names – PAVEL and LAZLO. It did not take him long to work out how they got there.

"Good girl, Donna! We'll find you."

The hasty exit from the farmhouse had left all four of them jangled. They had driven away at speed in a battered Skoda and were now over fifty miles from their original hideout. Their second refuge was a disused warehouse that made the farm look like a three-star hotel. It was cold, dark and full of strange echoes. Emilie was taken off by Pavel to make the telephone call to the Czech Embassy then she and Donna were allowed to curl up in the corner of a storage space at the top of the building. They were given nothing more than an old blanket to keep them warm and they huddled closely together. Pavel and Lazlo took it in turns to sleep so that one person was on permanent guard. It was a long night.

Donna awoke to the sound of rain. She was aching all over and groaned as she stretched herself. Emilie was already awake, listening to the patter on the roof. They had been far too fatigued to talk during the night and they were under such close supervision. Lazlo was now watching them from some twenty yards away. They were free to compare notes.

Emilie squeezed her friend's arm.

"Donna?"

"I think . . . I know why?"

"Do you?"

"Last night . . . I speak telephone?"

"Who did you talk to?"

"The Embassy in London."

"What did you say?"

"What they tell."

"Pavel and Lazlo?"

"Yes. I okay . . . but please help me soon."

"Then what?"

"Lazlo speak . . . not hear all but he say prisoners."

"Prisoners?"

"Back home, maybe . . . In Prague."

"I see," said Donna. "They want to make a trade. Emilie Deltchev for the release of some prisoners. That's why they chose you."

"Me?"

"You're one of Czechoslovakia's best assets."

"I no . . . understand."

"It helps them to put on real pressure."

Aware that they were chattering away, Lazlo got up and came lumbering across to them. He had had a broken night as well and was in need of a shave. His English was more limited than Pavel's.

"You – no talk."

"We're hungry," complained Donna.

"Breakfast . . . soon."

"And we're freezing. We need more blankets."

"No . . . that all."

"Then we'll have to get ourselves warm," said Donna, getting up. "Come on, Emilie."

She took the girl by the hand and pulled her to her feet. Lazlo trained a gun on them and ordered them to sit down again but Donna waved him aside.

"Shoot us, if you want. We'd prefer that to being frozen to death. We're going to have some exercise."

And before the astonished gaze of her captor, she moved to the centre of the room and started to go into the warm-up routine that she used in gymnastics. Emilie smiled and ran to join her. The two of them were soon immersed in a set of exercises that warmed them up and made them feel much better about themselves. They were still prisoners but they were able to escape into the world of gymnastics for twenty minutes.

Alarmed at first, Lazlo soon relaxed and put his gun away. They were doing no harm. And it was entertaining. He was getting a private performance by one of the greatest woman gymnasts ever. It was quite inspiring.

He did not realize that the girls were doing far more than simply keep their bodies in trim. They were rebuilding their confidence. They had taken the initiative against their captor and got away with it.

Their hope flowered.

Maggie Melrose cancelled her appointments for the day and stayed at home. To fend off nuisance calls, she asked her father-in-law to take over as switchboard girl and Wilf despatched any unwanted callers with a few blunt words. Stuart hung around the house until midday then he went off to Hillcrest to see his father. As he was going in through the main door, Kim Davison ran over to him.

"Hello, Stuart."

"Hi."

"I was hoping I might catch you here."

"Shouldn't you be at school, Kim?"

"I've missed my lunch so I could pop over here."

"Got time for a snack?"

"If it's a quick one."

They went upstairs to the restaurant and found a table in the corner. Stuart bought them both a cup of coffee and some hot pasties. He liked Kim a lot but he was always a bit wary of her because she could be spikey at times. Today, she was very subdued.

"Any more news?" she said.

"Not yet."

"Poor Donna!"

"And Emilie. Must be awful for both of them."

"Yes. I just wish there was something I could do."

"You've done it by coming here, Kim. You've cared."

"Everyone's talking about it at Kingsmead."

"That's why I ducked out today."

"We've been besieged by reporters."

"So were we until we set Grandad on to them." Stuart managed a smile. "He may look old but he's as fierce as a Rottweiler when he wants to be."

"Donna, of all people! So unfair."
"She was in the wrong place at the wrong time."
"I feel so sorry for you all."
"Thanks," he said, touching her hand.

Kim munched a mouthful of pasty then washed it down with a swig of tea. She tried to sound casual.

"Tania Hancox was talking about you at school."
"Was she?" he said uncomfortably.
"Reckoned she was going to ring you up."
"Grandad will give her an earful."
"She claimed that you'd tell her anything."
"Did she?"
"Well, you know what Tania's like. Always shooting off her mouth about something. I think she's just jealous because someone else is getting all the attention.
"Yeah."

Kim finished her snack and sat back.

"Stuart . . . "
"Mm?"
"You're not her boyfriend, are you?"
"Tania Hancox?"
"That's what she was implying. Is it true?"
"Not really."
"Then why did she say it?"
"Tania is Tania . . . "

His shrug seemed to satisfy her. She leant over quickly and gave him an unexpected kiss on the cheek.

"I'd better go," she announced.
"Let me walk down to the front door with you."
"Right. And thanks for the meal."
"Any time."

Stuart was relaxed on the outside but his mind was

in overdrive. Not only was he distressed by what he had heard about Tania Hancox, he saw something that he had never even noticed before. Kim fancied him. He was not sure whether to be pleased or embarrassed.

He waved her off outside the front door and she headed back towards Kingsmead at a steady trot. In addition to everything else, the crisis over Donna had brought confusion to his love life. He was now having new doubts about Tania Hancox and second thoughts about Kim. It was all very confusing.

Stuart was about to go back into Hillcrest when he saw a man in a smart grey overcoat walking along the pavement. The hornrimmed glasses were unmistakable. It was the same man he had met on the stairs the night he smuggled Tania in to see the Czech gymnasts. Stuart was convinced that he was somehow involved in the kidnap and his first instinct was to jump on him and call for help. Instead, he let the man go past him then followed at a discreet distance.

It was not long before the stranger turned in through the main entrance of the Regency Hotel. That clinched it for Stuart. He ought to go to the police and tell them what he knew. Except that they would ask why he had not reported it before. His father would be dragged in and Stuart would have some hard questions to answer. What he needed was more to go on. The only way he could redeem himself was by doing some detective work on his own account. If he could hand the police some cast-iron evidence, then he might yet emerge as a hero.

Strolling into the hotel, he was just in time to see the man collect his key and go into the lift. He went up to the reception desk and addressed the young woman.

"Oh, excuse me. My uncle just came in."

"Mr Pendry?"

"That's him. Uncle Charlie. I'm supposed to meet him here. Can you tell me his room number?"

"Yes, sir. 416."

"Good. I'll nip up and surprise him."

"You can't do that, I'm afraid," she said politely.

"Why not?"

"Because we have a security alert at the hotel. No non-residents are allowed upstairs. If you want to speak to your uncle, use a house phone to call him."

She indicated a wall telephone on the other side of the foyer. Stuart went over and pretended to make a call. As soon as the girl at the desk was diverted, he slipped out of the hotel and crossed the road. Lounging in a doorway, he kept the hotel entrance under scrutiny.

The man had to come out again some time.

Stuart would wait. No matter how long it took.

He owed it to Donna.

Pavel drove back to the warehouse and hid the car out of sight of the road. He had brought some food for lunch and shared it out with the others. Donna and Emilie moved away to eat on their own. Lazlo wanted an update.

"Well?"

"I spoke to the ambassador himself."

"And?"

"He has been in touch with Prague. He says they are giving the matter top priority."

"When will they be released?"
"He made no promises."
"We must have action!"
"I made that clear."
"What if they don't obey our demands."
"We have to turn the screw a little more."
"How?"
"A severe warning."
"The English girl?"
"If necessary."

Lazlo glanced across to where the two girls were sitting on upturned boxes as they devoured sandwiches. Donna's presence was a nuisance in every way. In order to achieve their aims, she might have to be sacrificed.

His impatience made him punch his other hand.

"Why are they being so slow about it?"
"Playing for time."
"The longer we wait, the more chance there is of being caught."
"We're safe here," assured the other. "The police had a lucky break with the laundry van but they can't possibly trace us here. Besides, they haven't a clue who we really are."

Superintendent Jackson stared at the screen as the computer printed up details. The raid on the farmhouse had been a failure but it had delivered one bonus. The two names had been matched with those of known members of an extremist Czechoslovakian political group. Terezie Klimenko's descriptions of the two men had also been brought into play. The computer had done the rest.

Two names appeared on the screen.
Pavel Minaev and Lazlo Durdis.
Superintendent Jackson gave a grim chuckle.
"Got you, my lads!"

Chapter 7

Hillcrest had been trial by ordeal that morning and it left Cliff Melrose wearied. After the sticky interview with Viktor Zaremba, he had to field dozens of calls from people who had party bookings for the big event on the following day. Was it still on? Even as he assured them that it was, he began to have grave doubts. Pressure was constant and some of the calls were downright offensive. It was all very harrowing. The one bright ray of hope was extinguished by Superintendent Jackson when he rang for the second time. Cliff learned that the police located the hideout and the transit van but that there was no sign of the two girls. Without giving details, Jackson told him that they had found valuable clues but that did not assuage Cliff's deepening fears.

All he heard was one stark fact.

No Donna.

Weighed down by it all, he went off for his daily swim in the pool just before lunch. It revived him slightly but another cloud menaced. Harry Wyman was waiting for him with his usual blend of smugness and aggression. The Councillor pitched straight in.

"What's all this about going ahead?"

"We have to, Harry."

"In the middle of a major diplomatic incident?"

"It may all be over by tomorrow."

"Yes, and it may drag on for another week."

"You always were an optimist," said Cliff.

"Don't be sarcastic."

"Then get out of my hair."

"You have to cancel!" insisted the other.

"Who says so?"

"Commonsense."

"Never been very high on that, I'm afraid."

"The Czechs won't play ball without Emilie."

"I know that."

"So how do you propose to get her here? Are you going to wave a magic wand and pull her out of a hat like a white rabbit?"

"Harry," sighed Cliff. "If I had a magic wand, you would have disappeared months ago."

"It's going to be the other way around."

"How come?"

"You're going to do the vanishing act."

"Who says so?"

"My colleagues will," said Wyman with confidence. "When they hear what plans you have for Hillcrest, they'll wonder why they appointed you in the first place."

"And what plans are those?"

"Let's start with your rock-climbing scheme . . ."

Clife Melrose blanched. In order to diversify the appeal of Hillcrest even more, he wanted to provide some additional attractions that would bring in people who had never been near the place before. The construction of a practice wall for novice climbers was one such idea. It would bring in schools and youth clubs.

Harry Wyman poured scorn on the idea and treated the other long-term plans with equal derision. Cliff was put on the defensive. Some of his most cherished ambitions were being trodden under foot. Once again, he could not understand how the Councillor had got hold of so much inside information on Hillcrest. It was almost as if Cliff's office was bugged. Wyman had free access to the Director's innermost thoughts.

"I don't like it," concluded Wyman.

"That's your problem."

"It's also yours, Cliff. You were brought in here as a new broom. Instead of that, you're turning out to be a feather duster. Let me give you some advice."

"Stick it."

"Consider resignation."

"Never!"

"More dignified than being sacked."

"My contract still has several months to run."

"It can be terminated in special circumstances."

"You don't frighten me, Harry."

"Just wait. When you're forced to cancel tomorrow's event and people see how much this fiasco has cost us, you won't have any friends left at the Town Hall. Then there are these ridiculous plans of yours." Wyman smirked. "I have enough to crucify you, Cliff."

"Go ahead."

"That's just what I intend to do."

Cliff went across to yank the door open.

"Out! You've done your bad deed for the day."

"There's much worse to come."

"I'm shaking in my boots!"

He took Wyman by the arm and helped him through the door before closing it hard behind him. Then he sat on the edge of his desk and pondered.

With problems enough to worry about, he now had his whole future at Hillcrest under serious threat.

Where did the Councillor get his information?

Who was the traitor?

Stuart waited for two hours before anything happened. He was starting to get very tired and disconsolate at his post then Pendry emerged from the hotel. Dressed as before in his stylish overcoat, the man swung left and walked along the pavement. Stuart waited for the traffic to thin out then he crossed the road and followed his quarry. It was a busy time of day and so he was able to use the crowd as a camouflage. There was no chance that Pendry would know that he was being trailed.

The man walked briskly and seemed to know the area well, cutting up one street and turning into another. He paused at a newsstand to buy the lunchtime edition of the Evening Standard. As Stuart passed the stand himself, he saw a photograph of his sister on the front page beside a much larger one of Emilie Deltchev. It only served to stiffen his resolve and he pressed on.

Pendry turned another corner and Stuart broke into a jog to catch up with him. But he was not fast enough. When he stopped at the corner to peer round it, Pendry was nowhere to be seen. Stuart hurried along the street but to no avail. He had lost his man. Retracing his steps, he checked every shop and building to see if Pendry might have gone into them.

Eventually, he came to an alleyway. A sign on the wall indicated that it led to the British Legion. He saw the door at the far end and walked slowly towards it. As he passed a window, he heard muted sounds of chatter from within. Stuart had to stand on his toes to look through the window. All he could see was the tops of some heads.

In a flash, his vigil was over. Before he could do anything to defend himself, he was grabbed expertly from behind. His arm was twisted up behind him and he was forced hard against the wall.

The voice was cold and uncompromising.

"Why were you following me?"

It was Pendry.

Donna Melrose had been long enough in their company to work out the relationship between the two men. Pavel was obviously the leader. He was much more intelligent and decisive. It was Pavel who was handling the negotiations with the Czech Embassy. Lazlo was too impulsive for such a delicate task. He was essentially an action man who had dedicated himself to a political cause. Tough, fearless and single-minded, yet he had a softer side to him and the girls had exploited this when they did their gymnastic exercises. It created a bond with him.

The warehouse was very basic. It did not run to a bathroom with all mod cons. When the girls needed to relieve themselves, they had to use a filthy old toilet with a flush that did not work properly. It was along a corridor on the ground floor. What made it even more distasteful for the girls was that one of the men had to accompany them and stand outside the door.

Donna used her first visit for reconnaissance. By standing on the lavatory, she could peer out through the grimy window at the back of the cubicle. It showed her something that made her heart lift slightly. She could not wait to get back to Emilie to tell her the news.

The storage space was a three-sided room in the top storey of the building. It was large and gloomy with a pervading smell of dead fish. Donna joined Emilie in the corner where they sat together on orange boxes. She waited until the two men fell into conversation then she leaned over to whisper in Emilie's ear.

"Good news."

"Yes?"

"I had a good look around."

"Have you?"

"I found a way to get us out of here."

There was a limit. After several hours of giving unwanted callers a flea in their ear, Wilf Melrose signed off. Too much enjoyment was not good for him. He was a grumbler by nature and much more at home in that role. He took his leave of his daughter-in-law.

"I'm off now, Maggie."

"Hillcrest?"

"I'm playing bowls with Sam at four."

"Thanks for everything."

"You shouldn't be bothered any more," he said proudly. "I've seen most of the blighters off. They wanted a quote for their damn papers and I damn well gave one to 'em!"

Maggie opened the front door and glanced out.

"Dark clouds up there. Could be rain."

"Don't think so."

"Take an umbrella just in case."

"Can't be bothered, Maggie."

"You might regret it."

"Ha!"

Wilf Melrose set off down the street. Hillcrest was the best part of a mile away but he liked to walk there to give himself a daily constitutional. His route took him past Kingsmead and he glanced wistfully over at the school. His granddaughter should be in attendance that afternoon. Instead, she was being held captive somewhere by two men who were described as political activisits. That dismayed Wilf. Czechoslovakia was a Communist country and he distrusted left-wing agitators. They always went too far. It grieved him that Donna was in the hands of such volatile men.

The rain came without warning. Wilf cursed aloud and pulled his flat cap down over his eyes. As he trudged on towards Hillcrest, he was soon drenched by the downpour. He stepped into a shop doorway and waited until it eased off slightly then he continued his journey, picking his way through the puddles that had formed.

He was taking a short-cut through a sidestreet when calamity overtook him. A large car swept past him at speed and sent a fine spray all over him. He coughed and spluttered and waved his fist as the Rover came to a halt outside a house further along the street.

When the driver got out and waddled towards the house, Wilf's ire increased tenfold. His brandished fist became a cruder gesture.

The man was Harry Wyman.

Though fit and strong for his age, Stuart Melrose was no match for his assailant. He was guided in through the door of the club and down a narrow passage. Once inside a small office, he was released and pushed into a chair. He tried to rise but a strong hand shoved him down again.

Pendry loomed over him with controlled anger.

"Who are you?"

"I'm saying nothing."

"You trailed me from the hotel."

"No, I didn't."

"What's your game, sonny?"

"Guess."

Pendry studied him then snapped his fingers.

"I've seen you before."

"You must be mistaken."

"Hillcrest. Wednesday night."

"Not me, mister,"

"You were in the balcony with that girl."

"Must've been somebody else."

"Let's see, shall we?"

Pendry moved with such speed that his hands seemed like a blur. He grabbed Stuart by the lapels, slipped one hand inside his coat and extracted his wallet. It was being examined before its owner could voice a protest.

"Hey, that's mine!" exclaimed Stuart.

"I just want to know who I'm dealing with."

"Give it back."

Pendry found what he was after and returned the wallet. His anger softened and he was almost considerate.

"You're her brother, aren't you?"

"Whose?"

"Donna Melrose."

"Yes, I am."

"So that's why you chased after me."

"You were in on the kidnap!" accused Stuart.

"Unfortunately, I wasn't."

"We saw you at Hillcrest. Snooping around."

"Looking for the bar."

"Where's Donna?"

"I wish I knew."

"What have you done with her?"

"I've never even met your sister, Stuart. And if she's as aggressive as you, I'm not sure that I want to. Now, take it easy, will you?"

"Come clean," insisted the boy.

"About what?"

"Where are you holding my sister?"

"I'm not. That's the truth."

"You abducted her from the hotel."

"Do I look like a Czechoslovakian hothead?"

"I should have put the police on to you."

"That might not have been very wise."

"They'd put you away where you belong."

"I doubt it."

"You can't fool me," said Stuart. "Your name is Pendry and you were staying at the hotel so that you could pounce on Emilie Deltchev. Admit it."

"I'm admitting nothing. What I will do, however, is to show you something that might alter your view of me."

"Don't bank on it."

Pendry took out his wallet and opened it to flash a card under Stuart's nose. As he read it, the boy's mouth dropped wide open. Pendry smiled.

"Still want to turn me over to the police?"

They waited until Pavel went out. He was far too astute to be taken in by their plan. Lazlo was different. They had an outside chance with him. Donna chose her moment.

"Can we do some more exercises?"

"Why?"

"We're cold. And Emilie has to keep in shape."

"Stay there."

"What harm can it do?" said Donna artlessly.

"Sit down again."

"But Emilie was going to do her floor exercises."

"Her what?"

"She has to do them every day to maintain such a high standard. Normally, she has music, of course, but she's going to do them without today."

Lazlo thought it over. He was undecided.

"Why not let us do five minutes?" suggested Donna. "If it's boring to watch, you can always tell us to stop."

After a full minute, he gave a curt nod of approval.

They went straight into a shortened version of their warm-up routine. It took more than five minutes but Lazlo did not object. He was interested. The little performance broke up the tedium of guarding them.

Emilie Deltchev soon went into her floor exercises. Donna retreated to the corner of the room so that the gymnast had ample space in which to work. Emilie began with a run and two forward somersaults then she stood on one leg and bent over until her chin almost touched the floor. A twist and a few quick paces took her into a series of flic-flacs.

Lazlo was hypnotized. He had never seen such grace and vitality. Emilie pulled out all the stops, using the whole floor area to demonstrate her art. He was so caught up in her work that he did not notice Donna creeping up behind him with one of the boxes. With all the weight she could muster, she swung it against the back of his head and knocked him over. Without even daring to look back, the pair of them took to their heels and sped off down the stairs.

"This way, Emilie!" said Donna.

"I with you."

"Great work!"

"It your plan."

They saved their breath for a dash into a room that was directly above the toilet. Donna shut the door after them and rammed home the bolt. Lazlo had now recovered from the blow. They could hear him roaring away upstairs. There was no time to lose.

"Where now?" said Emilie.

"Through the window."

"We are too high."

"Look outside."

Donna swung open the steel-framed window to reveal an iron girder that ran to an adjacent building. It was very narrow but only about twenty feet long. If they could possibly get across it, they could descend by the fire escape on the other building then cross the canal by the bridge. Once over there, they could lose themselves in a warren of abandoned warehouses.

There were problems. It was drizzling and the girder was wet. Directly beneath it on the ground was a pile of old bricks. Any fall could result in serious injury. Then there was the crosswind.

Emilie took fright as she looked down.

"No like."

"Think of the beam," urged Donna.

"Beam?"

"This is almost the same thickness."

"Is . . . different."

Lazlo had now worked out where they were. He hammered on the door with his fist then resorted to kicking it. Emilie shook off her reservations.

"We go."

"I'll lead the way."

It was trickier than it looked. Donna's sense of balance was good but it was only ever demonstrated in a gymnasium where there was always a rubber mat to break her fall. Here she had to contend with the elements. One mistake might be her last. She kept her head up and felt her way along the girder with her feet. It seemed to take her an age to cross the small distance. When she reached the other side, she clutched the brickwork with relief.

Then she turned to beckon Emilie across. Once on the beam, the girl was far more assured. She tripped across without any hesitation and gave her biggest grin when she reached the other side. They shot down the fire escape and scampered towards the bridge over the canal. As they crossed the ugly slick of black water, they heard a loud bang behind them as the door finally gave way under Lazlo's attack. He would never catch them now. They had too big a start and the cover of more buildings.

"We've done it, Emilie!"

"Yes, yes!"

"Keep running."

"We . . . away."

"I knew it would work."

"Where . . . go?"

"Down here!" said Donna.

She turned into a gap between two buildings and tore down it with Emilie at her heels. Freedom lent them wings and they fairly tore over the ground. Lazlo's voice was now just a distant echo. They had fooled him completely.

They swung left in front of one building then darted down another alleyway. But this time they made the wrong choice. Their way was blocked by a car and they came to a dead halt. It was the Skoda.

Pavel was leaning against it with his gun out.

He gave them a quizzical smile.

"Where do you think you're going?"

Chapter 8

Left on her own in the house, Maggie Melrose found that she was brooding continuously. She could not get Donna out of her mind and her fears for her daughter's safety increased with each hour that passed. In the end, Maggie elected to go over to Hillcrest to join her husband. At least they could offer each other support if they were together. Being alone made her prey to the most dreadful thoughts. They had to be kept at bay somehow.

Wearing his usual track suit, Cliff was standing in the middle of the sports hall, gazing round sadly at the gymnastic equipment. The biggest event he had organized since taking over as Director was now on the verge of collapse. He glanced up at the empty banks of seating.

Maggie read his thoughts and held his hand.

"It might still happen, Cliff."

"Pigs might fly."

"We mustn't give up hope."

"I know, love. And I haven't." He kissed her gently on the forehead. "Anyway, what's a gymnastic international compared with the safety of a daughter? I'd be happy to see Hillcrest burned to the ground right now if it would bring Donna back to us."

"If only we had some news."

"The police are doing all they can, Maggie."

"They don't seem to have made any progress," she

said despondently. "I listened to every bulletin on the radio. They're still no nearer to finding her."

"That's not true. I'm sure they've made headway."

"Then why don't they say so?"

"Because they have to be very careful how much they release to the media. The kidnappers will have a radio as well, you know. The police don't want to warn them how close they're getting."

"Do you really believe that, Cliff?"

"We have to, love."

She nodded then turned to survey the empty hall.

"It's so unjust!"

"I'd use a stronger word than that."

"You sweated blood to set this event up."

"Don't remind me."

"I suppose there's no hope of a postponement?"

"None at all, Maggie," he said. "If it doesn't take place tomorrow, that's it. I'd never be able to persuade the Czech team to come near the place again." He gave a mirthless laugh. "Not that it would be up to me."

"What do you mean?"

"Councillor Harry Wyman."

"Oh, no!"

"He's been around here to gloat."

"The vulture!"

"If this venture fails, Hillcrest will not only lose money and credibility. It will lose its Director."

"They couldn't do that to you, surely?"

"They could and they will, Maggie," he admitted. "Wyman is really gunning for me. I don't know who tipped him off, but he's got hold of lots of information that he wasn't supposed to have. Sensitive information."

"What are you saying?"

"This could be it. Wyman has me over a barrel."

Maggie was horrified. She had not forgotten what it was like to have her husband out of work. Hillcrest had been a godsend and he had been very happy there until now. If Cliff were forced to leave under a cloud, he would find it much more difficult to find another job. Before she could offer him sympathy, they were interrupted.

Standing in the doorway was the ample figure of Superintendent Jackson. His tone was non-committal.

"I wonder if I could have a word in private?"

The afternoon had brought him nothing but aggravation. After being soaked by the passing car, Wilf Melrose was stopped at Hillcrest by a security officer who asked him to show some proof of identity before he was let in. It was in vain that the old man argued that his own son was the Director of the place. Since the kidnap, security at Hillcrest had been stepped up even more and nobody was immune. A final crushing blow awaited Wilf. Instead of finding solace on the bowling green by beating his opponent, he was unaccountably off form and lost easily.

Disappointment sent him off to the restaurant for a consolatory cup of tea. Stuart Melrose bumped into him in the corridor.

"Hello, Grandad."

"It's an insult."

"What is?"

"To lose to someone like him. Any other day of the week, I could wipe the floor with him."

"You've lost me," said the baffled Stuart.

"That car."

"Eh?"

"Rover."

"Could you try talking in English?"

"That's what put me off my stroke."

"Stroke?"

"On the bowling green. Don't you understand, lad?"

"Not a single word."

"When I was walking here in the rain, this black car shoots past me and almost drowns me. And who should be driving it but Mr High-and-Mighty himself."

"Who's that?"

"Councillor Harry Wyman."

"Oh, him!" said Stuart. "Dad's big headache."

"He's my big headache as well," said Wilf tetchily. "But for Wyman, I'd have won that game of bowls. What really narked me was that he didn't even apologise."

"Probably didn't know he'd splashed you."

"Of course, he did. When he got out of his car, he saw me. But did he stop and say sorry? Not a chance! He went into that white house at the end of Radford Street."

Stuart Melrose reeled slightly.

"Radford Street?"

"That's where it happened."

"Was the white house number twenty-nine?"

"How should I know? It's the one on the left just

before you turn into Cameron Road. The point is that he ignored me completely. I should have gone after him and given him a piece of my mind. Shall I tell you what I think about Harry Wyman . . . ?"

Stuart was not listening. He was suffering the pangs of disillusion. He knew the house in Radford Street all too well. He still nourished faint hopes of going there on Sunday. It shocked him to learn that Harry Wyman was on visiting terms at the house. He knew just how much the Councillor hated his father. The seed of suspicion was planted in his mind and it grew swiftly.

He had been at the house only the night before.

Tania Hancox lived there.

Superintendent Jackson put the photographs side by side. Cliff and Maggie studied them with a mixture of curiosity and apprehension. They were in the Director's office. The door was locked against any intrusion.

"Who are they?" asked Cliff.

"The one with the beard is Pavel Minaev," said the detective. "His mate is Lazlo Durdis."

"What do you know about them?" said Maggie.

"Quite a lot, Mrs Melrose. They're both Czech exiles. Members of an extremist group that's based in Prague. It was formed in the wake of 1968."

"Wasn't that when Dubcek was ousted?" said Cliff.

"That's right. Dubcek was far too liberal for the Russians. When he became President of Czechoslovakia, the people were given dangerous things like civil rights. The Russians wouldn't allow that. So the army moved in, Dubcek was forced out and a stronger regime was imposed."

Maggie looked down at the photographs again.

"These two are much too young to have been involved in all that, surely?"

"They were, Mrs Melrose. But like all Czechs, they've had to suffer the consequences. I know that Gorbachev's been banging the drum about glasnost and perestroika in the Soviet bloc but Czechoslovakia has seen little of either. There's still the same oppression." He picked up one of the photographs. "Pavel Minaev knows all about it. His father was a civil rights leader. Until they locked him up. Otto Minaev has been in prison since 1968. He's one of the six people whose release is being demanded."

Cliff took the photograph from him to examine.

"So Pavel has a personal stake in all this?"

"Very much so."

"Ironic, isn't it?"

"What, Mr Melrose?"

"In any other situation, I'd be on his side. I hate what happened in Czechoslovakia. Reminded me of Hungary when the Russians crushed the uprising there. I support anybody in a fight for freedom." He heaved a sigh. "If only Donna hadn't been dragged into it."

"Most unfortunate, sir."

"But you say she told you their names?"

"We believe so. They were written on a wall."

Superintendent Jackson did not tell them that the information had been put there by a foot. He did not want to cause them unnecessary pain by explaining that their daughter probably had her hands tied behind her back.

Maggie Melrose pointed to the other captor.

"What about him?"

"He's more of a problem, I'm afraid."

"In what way, Superintendent."

"Pavel is a true political activist. It's his whole world. Lazlo Durdis is a more recent convert. He's in it for the excitement. We can rely on Pavel to keep his cool but Lazlo might crack under pressure. There's no knowing what he'd do then."

Cliff and Maggie exchanged an anguished glance.

Donna was in greater danger all the time.

Lazlo Durdis paced up and down the room, ranting wildly and pointing to the blood that was oozing from the wound on the back of his hand. It took Pavel Minaev a long time to calm him down. Watching it all from the other side of the room, Donna Melrose and Emilie Deltchev were taut and frightened. Their escape plan had been foiled and there would be repercussions. Lazlo jabbed an angry finger in the direction of Donna. She did not need a translation of what he was saying. It was patently clear.

Pavel rounded on the two girls. He grabbed Donna by the wrist and pulled her towards the door. Emilie shouted a protest in Czech but it went unheeded. Donna was taken down the stairs and along a corridor.

"What are you going to do with me?" she asked.

"You'll soon see."

"We'll get out somehow."

"Don't even think about it," he warned. "You're

a very lucky girl. If I'd let Lazlo have his way, you'd be lying on the bottom of that canal by now."

He kicked open a door and took her into an empty office. Like the rest of the warehouse, it was filthy and noisome. A thick metal pipe stood against one wall and bent at a right angle to run parallel with the ceiling. It was rusty and peeling but it had a use in the present situation. Pavel took some rope from his pocket and tied it to one of Donna's wrists before slipping it behind the pipe to secure her other wrist. Hands behind her, she was now trapped. He increased her discomfort by taking out a handkerchief and using it to gag her.

"That should keep you quiet."

Donna's yell of rage was muffled.

When Pavel went out, he locked the door behind him. He was taking no chances this time. Donna was being separated from Emilie for good. It was the Czech girl who was being used in their negotiations.

Donna had been shut away and forgotten.

They might never find her.

Terezie Klimenko had been very subdued since the kidnap. She was filled with remorse over what she saw as her own failure. Protecting the girls was her responsibility. She had never had any trouble before. But there was another reason for her sadness. She was very fond of Emilie and admired her gymnastic skills immensely. Terezie would be extremely sorry to lose her little friend but, one way or the other, that was now on the cards.

"Why are the police so slow?" said Viktor.

"Give them time," she said.

"They've had almost twenty-four hours."

"Emilie could be anywhere."

"Mr Melrose assured me she would be found."

"She will be. If she is still in England."

"What do you mean, Terezie?"

"We have to consider everything."

Viktor Zaremba had been stalking around his hotel room like a tiger in a cage. He stopped to sit down opposite Terezie. They had worked together for a number of years now and her advice was usually sound.

"What should we do?" he asked.

"Wait and see."

"Cancel tomorrow?"

"You cannot do that. You gave your word."

"I stand by it."

"Meanwhile, we must just hope that Emilie is found and brought back. She is very special to us all."

"How are the other girls?"

"Deeply upset. And restless."

"That can't be helped."

"It can, Viktor."

"How?"

Terezie shrugged. "It is not my place to interfere. You and Ludmila are in charge. I accept your decisions."

"Let me hear your opinion."

"It is not important."

"It is to me. Please."

The woman inhaled deeply through her nose.

"It is wrong to keep the girls penned up here at the hotel. They are young and fit. They need exercise. It is not healthy for them to sit around and think about

Emilie all the time. They are gymnasts. They should have the discipline to put everything out of their minds that gets in the way of their performance."

"There's something in what you say."

"Let them have a practice session, Viktor."

"We're not going to Hillcrest without Emilie."

"Then do it here."

"At the hotel?"

"They have a large banqueting room. It will be perfect. It even has mirrors down the walls so that the girls can see themselves and watch their mistakes. An hour in there would do them the world of good."

"It might help us all," he agreed. "But how do we know the management will let us use the facility?"

"I took the liberty of asking them."

Viktor smiled. Terezie always made noises about not interfering but she had a real influence on the way that things were run. Once again, he deferred to her wisdom.

He crossed quickly to the door.

"I'll go and see this banqueting room for myself."

"Shall I tell the girls to get ready?"

"Please, Terezie."

He was about to leave when he noticed the book lying by her bedside. It was a primer on Colloquial English.

"Where did you get that from?" he asked.

She was tempted to tell him the truth but something made her conceal it from him and she did not know why.

"It's mine," she said.

"Brushing up on your English?"

"Yes, Viktor. That's all."

Stuart Melrose was shaken. He had been forced to question his judgement of character. Convinced that Pendry had been involved in the kidnap, he was forced to accept that the man had no part in it. Exactly what Pendry was doing at the Regency Hotel he did not know because he had been given no real explanation, but Stuart now saw that he had jumped too quickly to conclusions.

It was the same with Tania Hancox. Desperate to become friends with her, he had been too ready to accept her at face value and to believe that she was genuinely fond of him. A stray remark from his grandfather made him think more carefully about her.

He adjourned to a telephone booth and dialled a number. Kim Davison answered and became excited when she heard his voice.

"What's happened?"

"Nothing."

"No fresh developments?"

"Not yet, I'm afraid."

"Oh."

He could feel the weight of her disappointment. She was a true friend to Donna and was finding the wait both irksome and unnerving. Stuart warmed to her.

"Kim . . ."

"Yeah?"

"Can I ask you a favour?"

"What is it?"

"Well . . ." Embarrassment made him hesitate.

"That means it's about Tania Hancox."

"It is, actually."

"I'm not giving her any message for you."

"Nothing like that, Kim."

"Then what?"

"You know her better than I do."

"Stop beating about the bush, Stuart."

"Okay," he said. "Does Tania have any connection with Harry Wyman?"

"Who's he?"

"A Councillor. Fat, oily man. Always getting his picture in the local paper. Know who I mean?"

"Not really."

"Then you can't help. Sorry."

"Wait a minute," she said as something was triggered off in her memory. "On the Council, is he? Tania did boast about him once. If it's the same man, that is."

"What did she say?"

"That her uncle would be the next Mayor."

"That's him," said Stuart. "Uncle Harry."

He thanked Kim and rang off, pausing to let the ugly truth sink in. No wonder Tania Hancox had been so keen to hear about the plans for Hillcrest. Her uncle probably set her up to it. Stuart was seething. Instead of taking out a girlfriend, he had been sitting in the back row of the cinema with an informer.

Waiting until he felt more composed, he dialled another number and asked for Tania. When she came on the line, she was dying to know the latest news.

"Nothing to report as yet," he said.

"Oh dear!"

"Nothing I can say over the phone, anyway."

"Then there is something?"

"Any chance of seeing you, Tania?"

"Tonight?"

"Yeah. Later on."

"I could manage an hour."

"Around nine?"

"Fine."

"I'll come to the house to pick you up."

"Uh, no," she said defensively. "We've got visitors. Better if we meet somewhere else. That coffee bar?"

"See you there at nine."

"Great!"

Any doubts he had were now extinguished. Tania was keeping him away from her house for one reason. Uncle Harry was there. They were definitely working together.

Stuart Melrose felt remarkably calm.

He knew exactly what he was going to do.

The important thing was never to give in. That would be fatal. Donna told herself that she must not resign herself to the worst. There simply had to be a way out of her predicament. She struggled hard to loosen her bonds but the rope was tied expertly. There was, however, a fair amount of play. Almost a foot of rope stretched between her wrists. That might be her salvation.

The pipe ran across the room some six inches below the ceiling. It was supported by a few metal brackets that had rusted with age. Donna noticed how sharp and jagged their edges were. A plan formed in her mind.

First of all, she kicked off her shoes. Then she leaned forward and pulled hard until she got maximum tension on the rope. Donna put one foot on the wall behind her, stabilised herself, then lifted the other. She was now completely off the ground, staring down at it with her whole body taut and strained.

Now came the real test. By jerking her wrists, she moved the rope a couple of inches and adjusted her feet accordingly. Her plan was working. It was a long, slow and agonizing ascent and the perspiration was soon dripping from her but she pressed on, ignoring the chafing of the rope on her wrists. She had never been so grateful until that moment for her gymnastic ability. All those hours of training under the supervision of Jane Ryder had made her fit, lithe and determined. Donna had to call on those qualities now and she crawled up the wall like a giant spider. Whenever she felt fatigue setting in, she thought about Emilie and gained fresh impetus.

It was an age before she reached the bend in the pipe. This was one of the trickiest parts of the whole manoeuvre. When the rope was finally jerked above instead of behind her, she forced herself into a slow motion forward roll that left her hanging down. With the last of her energy, she swung her legs up and around the pipe so that she could give herself a rest. She clung there for several minutes until her strength began to flow again.

It was now time for the final part of the plan. Donna inched her way along the pipe to the first bracket and flicked the rope over it. The hemp was now in contact with a sharp edge. She rubbed it to and fro in an effort to cut through it and got a mouthful of rust for her pains. But she was not deterred. Though she was aching in every muscle, she urged herself on until she could feel the strands parting.

When her energy was drained again, she let her legs drop so that the rope bore her full weight. She began to swing as if from a trapeze, putting additional strain on her bonds. Donna was putting herself through torture but it eventually paid off. The rope suddenly parted and she dropped down to the floor, landing with cat-like agility before sinking down to rest. She lay panting for over a quarter of an hour before she was able to move again.

A tired smile of triumph came.

She was free.

Chapter 9

Police activity on the case was intense. Pavel Minaev's address was located and his flat in Balham was raided. Among the things which were revealed was his ownership of a 1983 Skoda. Details of the car were flashed around the country. A garage attendant in Hampshire remembered serving petrol to a bearded man with a battered Skoda. The customer had spoken with a foreign accent and asked the whereabouts of a nearby farm. Shown a photograph of Pavel Minaev, the attendant was fairly sure that he had been the man. He did not know at the time that he was directing the Czech to the farmhouse used as a hideaway immediately after the kidnap.

Lazlo Durdis had been living in a bedsitter in Hackney. The police raid turned up an array of weapons, some live ammunition, some political pamphlets in Czech and some scribbled notes on a scrap of paper. When a translator was brought in, he identified the writing as a route to Southampton. This information coincided with the reported sighting of a dented Skoda, parked in a lay-by just outside Eastleigh the previous night. A lorry driver had seen two men changing a tyre on the vehicle as his headlights raked past them.

That narrowed the search at once. Everything was concentrated on Southampton. Road blocks were set up and the port was saturated with extra policemen.

Shops and supermarkets were checked to see if any of them recalled serving either of the two men whose photographs were now being shown all around the city. Three possible sightings of Pavel Minaev were recorded.

They were definitely in Southampton.

The net closed in.

Pendry was annoyed that Stuart Melrose had followed him but he believed he had shaken the boy off for good now. Telling him enough to get rid of him, Pendry yet gave away nothing of importance. Stuart had gone away from the British Legion Club at once reassured and mystified. That was Pendry's style. His charm could talk him out of most situations and he never conceded anything. In his line of business, it paid to keep your cards close to your chest.

He was in his room at the hotel when the call came.

"Hello."

"It's me," said his assistant.

"What gives?"

"You've got to meet a plane at Heathrow."

"From Paris?"

"Arrival time 1830 hours."

"Can't you do that?"

"They insisted on you."

"There's not much point, is there?" said Pendry with some exasperation. "We can't deliver the goods yet."

"That's what I said."

"And?"

"Meet the plane, anyway."

"I don't like anyone looking over my shoulder."

"Only one passenger."
"Male?"
"Female."
"That's worse."
"Ring here when contact is made."
"Right."
"Good luck."

Pendry put the receiver down and shook his head in irritation. He had enough to do without meeting planes from the airport and he was very unhappy about the arrival of this particular passenger. It complicated matters. But orders had to be obeyed.

Ten minutes later he hailed a taxi in the street.

"Where to, Guv?"
"Heathrow."
"No problem. Hop in."

The Melrose family sat in their living room and ignored the quiz programme on their television. Wilf did most of the talking, complaining like mad about everything and threatening at least six times to write to his Member of Parliament on this or that issue. In reality, he had no idea who his MP was. They all knew that. They also knew that his enthusiastic grumbling was only a smokescreen for the deep anxiety he felt about his granddaughter. It was his way of saying how much he feared for Donna.

Stuart was on tenterhooks when his father talked about Hillcrest. As Cliff talked about his collision with Harry Wyman, the boy's cheeks began to smart. Stuart had been very indiscreet. His careless remarks to Tania had landed his father in real trouble. The only atonement he could offer was to stage a rescue operation.

"I'm off out now," he said.

"Where?" asked his mother.

"Over to Martin's house. Just for an hour."

"Wouldn't you rather stay here? In case of news."

"Let him go," said Cliff. "Might take his mind off it. No point in all of us sitting in a circle."

"Thanks, Dad," said Stuart.

And he slipped out before there was any comment.

The quickest way to the coffee bar was straight along the main road but he made a detour so that he could go down Radford Street. The black Rover was still parked outside Tania's house.

Uncle Harry was in residence.

Stuart loped off to the coffee bar and arrived in time to stop two youths moving in on Tania Hancox. She had taken even more care with her appearance than usual and he had to fight against a surge of affection. He reminded himself of the black Rover and all was well.

Like everyone else, Tania was eager for news.

"What's happened?"

"Nothing much."

"Have the police found them yet?"

"Tell you in a minute."

He bought two coffees then nestled beside her at the table. Her face was a picture of innocence. Her fragrance was very alluring. It was difficult to believe she was capable of such double-dealing but he knew that she was.

"Well?" she pressed.

"Anything I say is strictly between us."

"Of course."

"It must go no further, Tania."

"You can trust me."

"I know," he said, squeezing her hand.

"Come on, then."

"The police know who they are."

"Who?"

"I can't reveal their names."

"Do the police say where they are?"

"They've got a pretty good idea."

"Where?"

"On the coast. That's all I can tell you."

"Is there any word of Donna?"

"None."

"But they think she's still with Emilie?"

"We hope so."

"And if she isn't?"

Stuart was not ready to go in for any ghoulish speculation about his sister. If Tania were given her head, she would have Donna beaten, assaulted and even murdered. Those were options that Stuart was just not ready to consider.

"Let's leave it there, shall we?" he said firmly. "It's very harrowing to talk about. And that's not the reason I wanted to see you tonight."

"Then what was?"

"What do you think?"

He gave her a wicked grin and she giggled. Tania liked to exert her pull over her boyfriends. Skilled in deception herself, she was not so quick to spot any deception played on her. As far as she could see, Stuart Melrose was still the same gaping admirer he had been on their first date.

"What was school like today?" he asked.

"We got invaded by the media."

"They're like an army of occupation."

"One of the reporters interviewed me," she boasted. "I told them how well I knew Donna and what a popular girl she was with all of us."

She told lies with effortless ease. He had to give her that. Nobody would guess that she loathed his sister and had gone out of her way to humiliate Donna at school.

They worked their way through various snippets of gossip then the talk turned to Hillcrest once again.

"One thing I didn't tell you last night, Tania."

"What's that?"

"Dad's best idea. It's fantastic."

"Is it?"

"I think so."

"Tell me."

"Only if you swear to keep it a secret," he said. "The contracts have only just been signed. Dad would kill me if he knew I'd let the cat out of the bag."

"I won't tell a soul, Stuart."

"Honest?"

She kissed him full on the lips. It was good.

"Now do you believe me?"

"Wow!"

"So what's this fantastic idea?"

He beckoned her closer and lowered his voice.

"A pop concert."

"At Hillcrest?"

"Yeah, in the sports hall. Great acoustics and if we pack everyone in, we could get three or four thousand. Dad's got some top groups coming – the Bangles,

Living in a Box, Bananarama. Might even get New Model Army."

"Sounds wonderful," she agreed. "But I thought Hillcrest was supposed to be a sporting venue and nothing else. Is your father allowed to run a pop concert?"

"Not really but he's going to stick his neck out."

"Why?"

"To convince the fuddy-duddies on the council that Hillcrest can be made to pay. Dad says that it's an under-used resource. He wants to broaden its appeal in every way. A pop concert is only the start."

"I see."

"Will you come with me, Tania?"

"Yes, sure."

"Free seats. Front row."

"Lovely."

"Just keep quiet about it, that's all. Dad's got the groups signed up but they've all agreed to say nothing until he springs the announcement. By then, it will be too late to stop him."

"As you say, he's taking an awful risk."

"Can't fail," said Stuart buoyantly. "The day that concert is advertised, the tickets will sell out. It'll be the biggest thing Hillcrest has ever done."

Tania's eyes gleamed with anticipation.

How much money was this scoop worth?

Emilie Deltchev was close to tears. Without Donna to bolster her morale, she felt totally intimidated. It was evident that the demands of the kidnappers had not met with an instant response and that made them angry. If they were refused altogether, they could easily become vengeful. Where would that leave her and Donna?

Pavel noticed the puckered little face.

"You must wish you'd never come to Britain."

"No," she said bravely.

"Despite what's happened?"

"I love this country."

"What about Czechoslovakia?"

"That's different."

He crossed over to her. She cowered.

"I'm not going to hurt you," he promised.

"When will you let us go?"

"When we get what we want. An answer from Prague."

"And if there is no reply?"

"There will be. They need Emilie Deltchev."

"I am not that important," she said modestly.

"Important enough to open prison doors."

"Prison?"

"Yes," he explained. "You must have gathered that we're going to trade you. For six political detainees. When they're given release papers and an exit visa from Czechoslovakia, we'll hand you safely back."

"What about Donna?"

"Never mind her."

"But she's my friend."

"Not any more."

Fully recovered from her exertions, Donna Melrose climbed through the window and shinned down the drainpipe to the roof. It gave her a chance to take proper stock of her surroundings. They were on the fringe of the dockland area. She could see ships in the distance. Gulls wheeled and dipped and drew lazy patterns in the grey sky. A siren went off. The tang of the sea got in her nostrils.

When she spotted some people about a hundred yards away, her first impulse was to attract their attention and get help. Then she remembered Emilie. Rescuing her had to be the main aim. Donna was going nowhere without her friend. They had been through so much together that a special bond had developed between them. It was a bond that had to be honoured.

Donna walked across the roof of the warehouse until she was above the section where Emilie was being held. To get her out would not be easy but she had one thing in her favour.

The element of surprise.

Pavel and Lazlo would not be expecting her.

She searched for a weapon.

The plane arrived on time and Pendry met the passenger in the Arrivals Lounge. Carrying her suitcase, he ushered her out to a taxi and they headed towards London. She wanted to be brought up to date with the latest news and he briefed her as they drove along. Her presence made him feel very uncomfortable because he was reminded of his failure. It was the only occasion in his life when his timing had been awry.

"Where are you taking me?" she said.

"The hotel."

"I want to go here."

"Where?"

She handed him a slip of paper. He read the name.

"I wouldn't advise it."

"Please. I ask a favour."
"It will only complicate matters."
"I must go, Mr Pendry."
"Why take such a chance?"
"Because I want to."
Her determination won the day. He capitulated.
"Very well. I'll take you there."

Harry Wyman had never parted with a ten pound note with more alacrity. He gave his niece an avuncular smile.

"How did you get all this out of him?"
"It's like taking candy from a baby," said Tania.
"Doesn't he suspect?"
"He's too stupid."
"Why do you go out with him, then?"
"I like him."
"Why?"
"That's the funny thing, Uncle Harry. I don't know."

Wyman had no time to plumb the mysteries of his niece's love life. She had given him a death warrant for Cliff Melrose. He could set the date of execution.

He rang the night editor on the local paper.

"Bernard?"
"Who is it?"
"Harry Wyman. Got something for you."
"I've heard that before."
"This time it's something really explosive."
"Your stories usually are."
"It's worth front page treatment."
"I'll be the judge of that, Harry."
"Okay, then, Listen to this . . . "

"Stop badgering me. I don't want to go to bed. Do I look tired? No, I'm full of beans."

"But you keep falling asleep," said Maggie.

"I close my eyes, that's all."

"It's getting late."

"I'm not quitting."

Wilf Melrose had nodded off several times in front of the television but there was no shifting him. He felt he had an emotional obligation to stay with the others, even if he was snoring away in his armchair. Maggie wanted him to go to bed so that she could be alone with Cliff. It was awkward for them to talk about certain things in front of her father-in-law.

Wilf grunted and dozed off once more.

"He's so cantankerous," said Maggie.

"Only just noticed?" Cliff managed a weary smile.

"How much longer must we wait?"

"You heard Superintendent Jackson. They're close."

"Not close enough."

"We don't know that."

"What if Donna has already been . . . ?"

But the question died on her lips as the front door bell rang. Wilf came awake with a start. Thinking it might be the police, Cliff and Maggie went swiftly out into the hall. The door was opened to reveal a middle-aged woman with a face that looked familiar. Despite her rather shabby clothes, she was poised and attractive.

When she spoke, it was with a heavy French accent.

"Mr and Mrs Melrose?"

"Yes?" said Cliff.

"I am Natalie Deltchev."

Maggie realised why the woman was so familiar.
"You're Emilie's mother."

Pavel was getting increasingly restive. His last call to the Embassy had convinced him that they were stalling for time. He arranged to ring back on the hour and got up now to return to the call-box. Lazlo intercepted him.
"This is their last chance."
"I'll handle the negotiations."
"You haven't done very well so far, Pavel."
"They know where we stand."
"Ram the point home."
"I'll give them an ultimatum."
"And if they don't meet it?"
Pavel flicked a cold glance at Emilie Deltchev.
"Then they lose their gymnastic champion."
He went down the stairs at speed. When he came out of the building and got into the Skoda, he did not see Donna Melrose watching him from her hiding place on the roof. She waited until the car was out of sight then she emerged from behind the parapet.

Donna unclasped her right hand. Lying in her palm were five small stones. They did not seem to be very effective weapons against a loaded gun.

Then she remembered David and Goliath.

Chapter 10

Stuart Melrose strolled home through the night and tried to be philosophical. His brief romance with Tania Hancox was at an end. She would soon come to realise that. In spite of everything, he suffered pangs of regret. Tania was still a very beautiful girl and nobody could leave her without experiencing some sense of loss. Even if it was pure calculation on her part, he had still enjoyed their time at the cinema. Tania was special.

On the credit side, he had got rid of her before she dropped him. That would be a blow to her pride. He had also avenged Donna and gone some way to make up for the embarrassment he had caused his father. Hillcrest was not just a workplace for Cliff Melrose. It was an extension of all their lives, the natural milieu for a family who had created their own sportsline across the generations. Stuart's folly had jeopardised everything. For a cuddle with Tania Hancox, he might have got his father sacked. He was right to ditch her.

As he turned into his road, he consoled himself with another thought. Tania was not the only girl at Kingsmead who liked him. The pressures of the last twenty-four hours brought a new contender out into the open.

Kim Davison. Bright, breezy, vivacious.

New fantasies began to form.

They vanished when he got within sight of his

home. A taxi was parked outside. Its engine was switched off and its driver was reading a newspaper by the light of the nearby lamp. Stuart was more interested in the man who sat well back in the rear of the cab. He felt that he knew that profile. When the light glinted on a pair of hornrimmed spectacles, he saw that he was right.

What was Pendry doing outside his house?

Natalie Deltchev was a small woman with a big heart and a readiness to help others. Even when she was agonising over the fate of her own daughter, she wanted to offer some sympathy to other grieving parents. She and Maggie Melrose had an instant rapport. Each understood exactly how the other felt. Both knew the suffocation that came from a sense of helplessness. They were drawn together.

Maggie Melrose had been amazed to see her.

"Did you come all the way from Czechoslovakia?"

"No," said Natalie. "From Paris."

"Ah."

"I was visiting relatives."

"Did you intend to come to Hillcrest tomorrow?"

"Hillcrest?"

"For the gymnastics."

"No," confessed Natalie. "That was not my plan."

"You may still get the chance," said Cliff bravely. "Emilie would never let down her public. When we get her back, I'm sure she'll want to take part in the event. You will be able to watch your daughter, after all."

"Maybe, Monsieur . . ."

There was a wistful note which showed that she did

not hold out much hope. Natalie Deltchev had not had an easy life. Hardship had etched deep lines in her face and made her look much older than she really was. He daughter's prowess had brought great joy but heavy responsibility as well. It did not sit lightly on her slender shoulders.

"I must go," she said, standing up.

"Stay as long as you like," offered Maggie.

"I interrupt long enough."

"Good of you to come," said Cliff.

"I had to see you, Monsieur."

"It meant a lot to us."

"Thank you. And to me."

Maggie escorted her to the door and pressed her to call again. Sharing their suffering had made it easier to bear. Natalie went off to the taxi and it drew away.

Stuart Melrose stepped out of the shadows and hurried towards the house. His mother let him in and they went into the living room together.

"Who was that?" he asked.

"Natalie Deltchev."

"Her mother?"

"That's right."

"She came here from Prague?"

"No. She was in France with relatives."

Stuart did some quick deductive work. The waiting taxi, Pendry, Natalie Deltchev. There could be only one logical explanation for it all.

"I think I know it, Mum."

"What?"

"The real reason why she came."

When Pavel went into the call-box, he had misgivings.

He organized the kidnap in the belief that it would produce an immediate result. Emilie Deltchev was the pride of Czechoslovakia. He thought that the government would do anything to get her back again. Instead of that, they were deliberately dragging their feet. What if they continued to do so? He knew in his heart that he could not bring himself to kill the girl. At the same time, he doubted whether he could stop Lazlo doing it. It was a dilemma.

He dialled a number and was put straight through. The ambassador himself came on the line. Pavel snarled into the telephone.

"Stop playing about with us!"

"We have not been playing," said the ambassador in a conciliatory tone. "We take this very seriously."

"So you should."

"But it is not something that can be rushed."

"We don't have much time."

"I explained that."

"You have been in touch with Prague?"

"Constantly."

"What is their decision?"

The ambassador cleared his throat before speaking.

"The release papers have been signed."

"For all six prisoners?"

"They will be free men within the hour."

"Exit visas?"

"Waiting for them at the airport."

"How do I know you are telling the truth?"

"I have a number for you to ring in Prague."

"Who will answer?"

"Your father."

Pavel felt a surge of emotion. They had won. All

the risks they had taken had now paid off. His father would be released from prison after all these years and join him in Britain. They would be able to fight for the cause together in exile. Pavel wanted to laugh out loud.

The ambassador was concerned with fine detail.

"And your side of the bargain?"

"Emilie is unharmed."

"When will she be returned?"

"When the six of them have flown out."

"How do we know we can trust you?"

"I gave you my word."

Pavel made a note of the number to ring in Prague then put down the telephone. He was overcome with relief. Expecting resistance, he had instead won everything that he wanted. Lazlo and he would be heroes.

He decided to rush back to the warehouse to pass on the good news but his way was blocked. Four men ringed the call-box. Pavel reached for his gun but they were armed as well. Four revolvers were trained on him.

Superintendent Jackson savoured his moment.

"Pavel Minaev? You're under arrest."

Patience was not one of his virtues. Left alone to guard their young captive, Lazlo Durdis became increasingly restless. He could not understand why his colleague was taking so long to make a telephone call. Pavel should have been back by now. It all made Lazlo very jumpy.

His edginess was infectious. Emilie caught it and watched him with growing disquiet. A man who loved action was trapped in a state of enforced inertia. He loathed it. He looked as if he would burst out of it at any moment and she might be his first victim.

Lazlo glared at her and tapped a foot on the floor. It was almost as if he were blaming her for what had happened. He wanted to exact punishment. Before he could decide what form it would take, his attention was suddenly diverted by a scream that echoed through the building.

It was Donna Melrose.

Laslo swung round with his gun at the ready. He charged off in the direction of the noise but could find no sign of her. As he peered along a corridor, something sharp and painful hit him on the back of the neck. It was the first stone and it inflamed him. Swinging round in a blind rage, he fired his gun down the corridor and the bullet ricocheted off the wall at the end.

It went nowhere near Donna.

Lazlo went rampaging up and down, searching every nook and cranny but she had disappeared into thin air. Another scream sent him darting down the stairs but she was still invisible. The second stone hit him on the top of the head and drew blood. Two more bullets were fired off wildly. The sound reverberated throughout the whole building. It was exactly what Donna had wanted. Gunfire would be heard outside. It was an alarm bell in itself.

Emilie was frankly terrified. With bullets flying all over the place, she flattened herself on the floor. Donna's voice called out to her.

"Don't worry, Emilie. I'm coming for you."

"Where are you?"

"Over here."

"Help me, Donna."

"Just wait."

Lazlo heard enough of Donna's voice to judge where it came from and he lunged off once more. This time a stone hit him in the face and produced a roar of anger. As he fired again, he heard the girl's mocking laugher. She seemed to be everywhere. He crept up the stairs again until he heard a bang to his left. Yet another bullet was wasted before he realised that he had fired at a metal door which had just been hit by a stone.

Donna was exhilarated now. She had studied the lay-out of the warehouse carefully before embarking on her game and she knew how to keep one step ahead of him.

"Come and get me!" she teased.

"I kill you!" he howled.

"I'm locked in here."

The voice seemed to come from the room where she had been tied up by Pavel. Racing across to it, Lazlo turned the key and flung open the door. The final stone was bigger than the others and it stunned when hurled from close range at the back of his head. As he reeled from the blow, two hands pushed him hard and sent him headlong into the room. The door was pulled shut and locked.

Donna went up the stairs like a flash of lightning.

"Quick, Emilie!"

"Where are we going?"

"Up and away!"

They went up a vertical steel ladder and gained access to the roof but they were not alone for long. The frenzied Lazlo shot the lock off down below and came after them with a vengeance. All thought of peaceful negotiation with the Embassy had gone out of his mind. He was after Donna Melrose now.

She would pay.

The planned exit had to be scrapped at the last moment. Descent down the fire escape was now no longer feasible. A man with a gun could pick them off from above. Their only hope lay in reaching the adjacent building. It was some eight feet away and a couple of feet higher. If they could somehow get on to its roof, they could duck down out of sight of Lazlo and scurry away. There was one major problem.

How did they get across the yawning gap?

Lazlo made that decision for them. As he came lurching out on to the roof, he fired yet again and the bullet was too close for comfort this time. It was Emilie Deltchev who responded to the emergency first. At the end of the roof was a four-foot parapet surmounted by a flat coping stone. She began her run-up.

"Vault!" she cried. "Vault!"

Getting up speed, she took off from the roof, hit the coping stone with both hands and did a perfect somersault before landing on top of the other parapet. It was quite inspiring. Donna prepared to follow suit.

It was her turn for the death vault.

Her options were not appealing. If she failed, she would plummet all the way to the ground. If she stayed where she was, Lazlo would get her. She summoned up all her courage and tried to tell herself that the coping stone was really only a vaulting horse and that the wide gap was no more than a couple of rubber gym mats.

Lazlo's next shot missed her by inches and set her off on her run-up. Emilie was standing on the next building, waiting to steady her, urging her on.

"Come on, Donna. You can do."

"We'll soon know."

She timed her take-off superbly and went up in a graceful arc. When she landed, her feet just reached the edge of the coping stone and she trembled for a second as if about to fall backwards. But Emilie caught her by the arm and pulled her down on to the other roof. They were safely behind the parapet when Laslo's last futile shot was fired. Hurling the gun after them, he built up speed himself so that he could go after them. He elected to jump up on the parapet and launch himself across the void but he was a foot short of his target.

The girls heard his blood-curdling yell before he hit the ground with a thud. The next sound that reached their ears was the wail of police sirens.

They were saved.

The nightmare was over.

There was joy unconfined in the Czechoslovakian camp at the return of their star. Emilie Deltchev got a rapturous welcome from all concerned. The reunion with her mother was tearful. They shared a room at the hotel so that they could be together. Emilie was shaken, bruised and very tired that night but she was in no way harmed. All that she needed was a long, restorative sleep. She was keen to compete next day at Hillcrest and was delighted that the event had not been summarily cancelled.

Viktor Zaremba rang to pass on the news.

"Thank you, Mr Melrose. You kept your word."
"With a little help from the police."
"And from your daughter."
"Donna?"
"Yes. Pity she is not Czech."
"Why?"
"Emilie tells me she is a natural gymnast."
"You can't get higher praise than that."
"Give her our warmest thanks."

Donna Melrose basked in the praise and tried to put aside the darker memories of her abduction. She was back home in the bosom of her family and that was all that counted. Cliff was glowing with pride, Maggie alternated between smiles and tears, Stuart was simply pole-axed with relief and Wilf slept happily through it all in front of the television. It was very late when they all went off to bed. Stuart and Cliff were the last to go upstairs.

"Goodnight, son."
"See you tomorrow."
"It's going to be a great day. I can feel it."
"So can I, Dad."
"Hillcrest has been saved."
"The enemy has been routed."
"Eh?"
"Buy the lunchtime edition tomorrow."
"What are you on about, Stuart?"
"Revenge," he said. "Read all about it."

Tania Hancox was still in bed when she heard the car screech to a halt outside the house. The bell rang, the door was opened and an irate voice came into the hall.

After sounding off down below, it came lumbering up the stairs. A puce Harry Wyman came barging in to throw a copy of a newspaper down on to the bed.

"Have you seen this, Tania?"

"I've only just woken up."

"Read it. Front page. Lead story."

"Why, Uncle Harry?"

"Just read it!"

She sat up in bed and glanced at the paper. Above a photograph of Cliff Melrose was a banner headline – POP GOES HILLCREST. Other photographs showed a line-up of famous pop stars. Tania was pleased.

"This is what you wanted, isn't it?"

"Until this morning."

"What do you mean?"

"The story isn't true."

"But I had it straight from the horse's mouth."

"You were conned, girl."

"Stuart wouldn't do a thing like that."

"No?" fumed Wyman. "Well, let me just tell you what's happened while you've been lying there having your beauty sleep. Cliff Melrose read this and threatened to sue the paper unless they print an immediate retraction. He's also taking me to court for spreading the libel in the first place."

He snatched up the paper and went to the door.

"Thanks to you, I've got egg all over my face."

"Didn't the newspaper check the story first?"

"Of course. Everyone denied it. But that's exactly what we expected because you told us it was being kept under wraps." He wagged a flabby finger at her. "Do me a favour, Tania, will you? Don't give me any more hot tips from your boyfriends. They're no good for my ulcers!"

He slammed out and left her dumbfounded.

She had been given her comeuppance at last.

Hillcrest was a cauldron of expectation that afternoon as a capacity crowd filled the sports hall. Picking up on the kidnap story, television cameras were sent along to record the highlights of the event and to give the venue some valuable free publicity. The stage was set for a scintillating display of gymnastics.

England acquitted themselves well but they were not in the same league as the Czech girls. The crowd were enthralled by the multifarious skills of the gymnasts from the Eastern bloc and none delighted them more than Emilie Deltchev. It was as if she were dedicating her performance to Hillcrest. She put everything into it and brought the spectators to their feet time and again.

On the beam, she was exquisite. On the asymmetric bars, she was sublime. During the floor exercises, she surpassed even her own high standards. But it was in the vault that she thrilled Donna Melrose the most. Running at the horse with a purposeful stride, she executed the identical vault that had helped them both to escape from Lazlo Durdis. On that occasion, the death vault had saved their lives. Here it brought a standing ovation.

Stuart was mesmerized. Sitting beside Kim Davison, he marvelled at Emilie's technique. She had everything. Strength. Stamina. Suppleness. Skill. And a style that was all her own. The girl was unique.

Her mother watched it all with pride and sadness.

Stuart noted that she was seated beside Pendry who seemed rather distracted. The boy soon saw why. When the event came to its climax and Emilie bore off the prize as the Individual Champion, a few people from the crowd rushed forward to congratulate her. Their example was taken up by others and the girl was soon engulfed. Pendry and Natalie Deltchev sidled unobtrusively away.

The crowd was now getting too large and excited. Terezie Klimenko waded in to rescue Emilie but the girl was not there. In the commotion, she had somehow taken the chance to sneak away. By the time the celebrations had died down, she had long since been whisked out of the building. This time she was a willing kidnap victim.

The spectators had not merely seen an Olympic champion at the height of her powers. Without realizing it, they had witnessed Emilie Deltchev's swansong.

She had bowed out.

The elation at the Melrose home that evening was mixed with regret. Donna was especially cast down to feel that her friend had fled from the world of gymnastics as well as from her own country. It seemed such a waste.

"No," said Cliff sagely. "Emilie quit at the very top even though she was only fifteen. How many other sports stars do that? She'd already conquered the Everest of gymnastics. There were no more peaks left to climb."

"The relief is that she performed at Hillcrest at all,"

said Stuart. "She was due to be taken out of the hotel by Pendry."

"Yes, who was that man?" asked Maggie.

"A former SAS colonel," explained her son, enjoying his moment centre-stage. "He was attached to the Foreign Office. The plan was to snatch Emilie and smuggle her across to Paris to join her mother. They'd both been promised political asylum there."

"How do you know all this?" said Donna.

"I don't. It's guesswork."

"Pretty sound guesswork," opined Cliff.

"The Czech team was thunderstruck," said Maggie. "They'd only just got the girl back and she was taken off again. It rocked them."

"It rocked me," admitted Donna.

"Oh, you haven't lost her," said her father. "When this has all blown over, I'm sure Emilie will get back in touch again. You saved the girl's life. Do you think she's going to forget that?"

"No, Dad. We'll always be friends now."

"Think of the other bonus."

"What's that?"

"You've got yourself one hell of a story for the school newspaper. Best exclusive they've ever had."

Donna Melrose brightened immediately.

"That's right," she said. "The very best."

RUN WITH THE HARE

LINDA NEWBERY

Elaine has to decide whether to run with the hare or hunt with the hounds – is she really committed to Animal Rights or is she more interested in Mark?

"It is a genuine novel, setting its interests within a satisfying context of teenage relationships and activities. The book is a good story, an intelligent argument..." *The Times Literary Supplement*

"Elaine is an intelligent and sensible heroine and by setting the romance in the world of Animal Rights, the author focuses attention on the adult world which appears confusing and often unfeelingly harsh to young people." *The School Librarian*

The
Sin Bin
series

KEITH MILES

1 Iggy   £1.95 ☐
2 Melanie   £1.95 ☐
3 Tariq   £1.95 ☐
4 Bev   £1.95 ☐

The Headmaster of Woodfield Comprehensive School cannot cope with troublemakers – so he sends them to the Sin Bin, a special annexe where all privileges are suspended and the pupils are under constant supervision. A spell in the Sin Bin was supposed to frighten pupils back into line, but instead it conferred on them a special status. They were heroes.

ARMADA

All these books are available at your local bookshop or newsagent, or can be ordered from the publisher. To order direct from the publishers just tick the title you want and fill in the form below:

Name _____

Address _____

_____

Send to: Collins Childrens Cash Sales
PO Box 11
Falmouth
Cornwall
TR10 9EN

Please enclose a cheque or postal order or debit my Visa/Access –

Credit card no:

Expiry date:

Signature:

– to the value of the cover price plus:

UK: 60p for the first book, 25p for the second book, plus 15p per copy for each additional book ordered to a maximum charge of £1.90.

BFPO: 60p for the first book, 25p for the second book plus 15p per copy for the next 7 books, thereafter 9p per book.

Overseas and Eire: £1.25 for the first book, 75p for the second book. Thereafter 28p per book.

Armada reserve the right to show new retail prices on covers which may differ from those previously advertised in the text or elswhere.

ARMADA